The Last Tourist in Bali

The Last Tourist in Bali

Watercolor illustrations by the author

Published by Baksun Books
ISBN 978-1-887997-39-3

This is a work of fiction. Any resemblance to persons living or dead is coincidental.

First Edition

the LAST TOURIST in BALI

stories

Tree Bernstein

For my editors

Timothy Lange and Jennifer Heath

Both of whom — at different times —
helped shape these stories

Table of Contents

Preface

In 2002, at the age of fifty, I left my home in Colorado and moved to the island of Bali. A couple of months after settling in the village of Kalibukbuk in the north, an Islamic group, Jemaah Islamiyah, set off bombs in Kuta, a nightclub district in the south, killing more than two-hundred tourists and Indonesians. By the end of the month nearly all the tourists had left the island. I decided to stay on, to take Indonesian lessons, and to learn the customs of this mysterious emerald green island.

I learned that the Balinese name their children according to birth order: the firstborn is Wayan, then Madé, Komang, and Ketut. The names translate as: First, Second, Third, and Fourth Child. Names do not indicate gender. (If there are more than four children, the fifth child is called Wayan Balik, or Wayan *Again.*) Nicknames are sometimes given, but family names are not. I met a lot of Wayans.

That was the year I did as I pleased—painted in the morning and swam in the ocean before lunch. I wrote stories that arrived as easily as the rain—they might begin with homestay gossip or village folklore. In Bali the spirit world and imagination walk the same path.

In my recollection, now eighteen years later, 2002 seems so long ago; a quaint, almost old-fashioned time. We had cellphones, sure, but people weren't so involved with them. You had to go to an Interenet Café to check email. Social media was unknown. I lived a couple of kilometers from the village at a guesthouse bungalow in a rice field that overlooked the Bali Sea. So much beauty ringed the island with a sleeping volcano at its heart.

One day, near the base of Mount Agung, that very volcano, I saw a girl in a bright sarong balance a bucket of water on her head as she came down the hill. The rising sun suddenly illuminated the red plastic bucket. For an instant the water turned into an animated cut-out, silhouetted like a shadow puppet that mimicked the sway of the girl's hips. She stepped out of the light back into shadow. The girl walked on.

Tree Bernstein
Boulder, Colorado

Pahon Pisang – Banana Trees

Passion Fruit

Raye sits alone at a table at the Sand Bar restaurant, but not for long. Stu rolls around the corner, shuffling into a drunken sailor's jig, a parody of a drunk. With a sweeping bow he doffs his cap and presents it to the waitress, who playfully puts it on her head. Stu snatches it back and demands a beer. He drapes one arm around the shoulder of another waitress and sings, "Today is my special day, la la la." Then he sees Raye. She waves. He weaves. He wobbles over to her table and plunks himself down.

"Today is the day I wear me hat and I don't give a fuck!" he boasts.

"What's the happy occasion?" asks Raye.

"Today is Anzac Day, what you would call Veteran's Day in the States. It's the one day of the year I wear me special hat." Raye looks closely at the baseball cap embroidered with a map of Australia and bars of various colors that represent medals.

"This hat must be very old."

"Right you are, mate, more than thirty years old. I wear it once a year on Anzac Day."

"It looks in pretty good shape," she says, but thinks, better shape than you are, my friend. Stu puts the cap back on his head and pours more beer into his glass. "To the war," he salutes with his glass and drinks. "I don't want to talk about it." Raye nods respectfully, but Stu goes on to tell her about hand-to-hand combat in Vietnam. Just had his twentieth birthday and there he was, getting knifed. He shows her the scars on his arms, ribs. "I don't want to talk about it," he says again. They drink their beers.

Three little Balinese boys and one girl step shyly into the restaurant. A woman, perhaps their mother, passes money to the waiter and leaves. The boys must be six or seven years old, the girl a head taller, a year older. They settle themselves into the wicker chairs, their chins almost level with the tablecloth. All grin widely as they enjoy the new sensation of acting like big shots at a fancy restaurant. The waitress brings two orange Fantas and portions it into four glass mugs.

Stu suddenly sobers up, taking in the scene along with other diners at the Sand Bar. The waitress serves one plate of fried rice to split between the four. They all talk at once, excited as baby birds. One boy notices the napkin-wrapped spoon and fork by his plate, holds up the prize and exclaims, *"barang-barang!"* Stu, all the waiters, and everyone who speaks Indonesian, laugh uproariously. The other three kids, who are digging into the rice with their fingers, pause, pick up the "silverware!" and, with great flourish, elbows pointing skyward, attack their supper with fresh enthusiasm.

The waiter tells Raye and Stu that the mother, who is nowhere in sight, is a rice seller at the beach. Three of the kids are her children, and one boy a friend of the family. Stu calls for another round of Fantas, which the kids slurp through straws with great gusto. They hum and bounce in their chairs to recorded music, grin and wave to friends passing by on the street. Stu asks, "Would they care for ice cream?" "Ya!" Their smiles grow even bigger. The waiter must go to a market around the corner for ice cream. The kids drum their fingers on the arms of their chairs and wait silently.

Each child has a different approach to eating an Eskimo Pie. One carefully picks off all the chocolate first; another comes in from the side. The girl delicately nibbles from top to bottom. One boy eats his in big bites, then watches sadly as his friends linger over their treats. They lick the ice cream sticks clean and pat their full bellies. Nothing more to say.

Stu heads to the restroom, but the kids wait for his return. When he comes back to the table, they all line up to shake hands with him and repeat "Thank you!" in English. They file out of the restaurant singing. It is suddenly very quiet.

Raye turns to face Stu. He orders a shot of arak. "Bloody Balinese, beautiful!" he says. They look at each other with matching smiles.

"That was sweet of you to buy them ice cream."

"Aw, it takes so little to make them happy. Too bad they have to grow up." Raye is just about to contest his statement when Sven saunters in. Stu's happy mood sours. He motions for another shot of arak.

A large, lumbering fellow, Sven fills the space. He is writing a Swedish-Indonesian dictionary. "It's never been done before," he informed Raye a month ago. She smiles at the idea of an Indo-Swede cultural exchange program. The Swedes get tropical fruit, sandy beaches, and clove-scented breezes; in exchange, the Indonesians get fjords and lutfisk. Sven works hard at his Indonesian, but no one can understand what he is trying to say.

"Why don't we just speak English?" asks Stu, exasperated. "We all understand that." Raye giggles. Sven wipes his sweating brow with a napkin and draws his fingers through his thinning silver-blond hair. He is almost finished with his first liter of beer and orders another. *"Degunt!"* he demands.

"That's *dingin,* mate, if you want your beer cold," says Stu, a little edge to his voice. "Fucking idjet," he hisses under his breath at Raye.

Sven, contrite and weepy, wants to talk. He had a fight with his girlfriend, got drunk, accused her of wanting his money. She took off to her sister's and he has not seen her in two days. "My beautiful Balinese girl," he laments. Stu rolls his eyes at Raye. When Sven goes to the restroom, Stu tells her the girlfriend is not Balinese. "She's from bloody Java and a whore, too. Just taking him for his money. The guy's an idjet."

Sven returns to the table, but forgets which language he is speaking, morphs into Swendonesian. He lights the wrong end of his cigarette, which Raye gently takes from him. Sven weeps about the fight. "It's all my fault, my beautiful Balinese girl, my darling." Stu has had enough, pays for his and Raye's beer, and takes his leave. Sven, new to Bali, is enchanted with everything exotic, especially the women. On his way around the world on a solo what-is-the-meaning-of-life trip, he fell in love with Bali and then, a Balinese girl. Well, maybe she was not born in Bali, but she lives here now, and she is young, so very young! She loves him, he is sure of it. He wants to marry this girl, but of course there is the matter of his divorce, and the house in Stockholm. Complications. Sven left his job as principal at a high school, as well as his three grown children and a loveless marriage endured for nearly forty years. Now he spends his days playing chess in the village and his evenings with his darling Balinese girl.

Raye halfway understands what he is saying, but it is an effort to want to try. When his chess partner shows up, she offers her seat at the bar and escapes. The night air is not cool, but it is a change from the cigarettes and beery breath of her incoherent companion. Suddenly, she misses someone far away.

The next day, Raye rises at dawn to explore the Lovina produce market. Along the dirt path hens follow their roosters to the fields. Some of the roosters are confined under airy basket domes. Raye wonders if they are to be sentenced to chicken soup or if their owners want more eggs than chicks. They are probably waiting for the afternoon cockfight. Sometimes she sees hens pecking around the rooster's cages, like wives visiting incarcerated husbands.

Next door to Raye's villa is a compound with small cinderblock thatched-roof huts and a large satellite dish. Farmers live here. Their docile caramel-brown cows have their own thatched hut, where they stand in muck all day to chew, chew, chew when not pulling or plowing. The mother cow looks up, startled when Raye stops to gaze at her black patent-leather nose with a rope drawn clear through. A shy calf hides behind her mother's rump. The cows are collared with large wooden bells that clack and thunk pleasantly when they pull the plow. Raye takes a soft pencil out of her satchel and makes a quick drawing of the two in her sketchbook.

Across from the neighborhood huts, a majestic villa looms large and ornate, owned by an American known affectionately in the neighborhood as Uncle. Workers recently completed a new *meru* with five tiers for the family altar. At full moon the gamelan orchestra played all day and into the night. Raye saw at least four priests and many offerings on the ground and in the high altars. A costly affair.

Along the path many small, indifferent, or cranky dogs watch her approach with suspicion. Raye sees a brown dog with a brown goose walking up the path together, conversing, or so it seems to her storybook eye. One family halfway down the road has a cart with chicken soup for sale in the early afternoon until dark, and another has a stand tucked inside their yard hung with various sundries, packages of unknown fried things, and bottles of soda pop. Raye has yet to see anyone buy anything, but people congregate there and sing out "*Selamat pagi!* Good morning!" from their gardens as she passes by.

At the end of the lane is a dirt lot filled with discarded plastic bags, bottles, cans, and smelly garbage festering under a shady banana tree. A real pigsty. Then Raye notices a lone little sway-back pig tied to the tree in the middle of the trash, the only clear spot in the whole mess. The pig grunts sadly to itself as it tries to nose rubbish just outside its reach.

The dirt road crumbles onto tarmac as Raye turns to the market under a great banyan tree in the center of the village. The crowded market has already sold out of steamed rice by the time she gets there at 7 a.m. She heads to stalls clustered in the corner with pyramids of orange, yellow, red, green, and purple fruit. With halting Indonesian, she manages to buy a few thin-skinned oranges, a fan of tiny pale-yellow bananas, and a huge mango—fruit she is familiar with. She knows she pays more than locals for produce, but feels shy about haggling over pennies for food.

Other produce she does not yet know by name wait to be claimed: jackfruit, bigger than a football with green knobby skin and distinct pungent odor; a small heart-shaped fruit that looks like a brown basket, that is astringent snakefruit; and *rambutan,* which looks intimidating with its furious red skin and wiry black hairs, but tastes as refreshing as a plum. She finds two kinds of passion fruit, one small and round that looks deceptively like a mottled orange, the other a big pale-green, squash-sized fruit that grows on a vine. She decides to avoid both, for now.

Entire tables are devoted to altar offerings. Piles of petals—blue hydrangea, orange marigold, some with their tiny petals separated into a tumble of gold, soft pink geranium, and papery bougainvillea in vivid purples, wait to be assembled into artfully woven banana-leaf baskets, always with a few long strands of curly petals from ylang ylang, which smells lemony and sweet at the same time. Raye holds out a 5000 rupiah note to the girl behind the counter who deftly assembles four baskets with some of each flower and a dash of oil that smells vaguely of men's hair tonic. Raye explains that she only wants one basket. The girl shrugs, puts the others aside but gives her a look as if to say, what good will that do? For the Balinese offerings must be given generously.

On the way back to the villa, people emerge from their homes for the early morning ritual of watering their entryways. Ducks waddle into the damp spots and squat in temporary ponds. The ducks are unbelievably ugly, but Raye thinks they would make a beautiful portrait with their mottled black and red warts, and orange beaks with big yellow ochre feet. In the back of a waiting pickup truck she sees a dead white hen collapsed as if sitting on a deflated nest, its eyes x-ed out, opaque. Raye begins to see animals as the Balinese do—as food, not pets. Even dogs are aware of this option.

Wayan sits back on his haunches and looks at the sun setting in the sea. He caught no fish today; his net tangled, then tore. His son had no luck finding tourists to transport on his motorcyle. No money today. His daughter sweeps the path in front of their house with sticks tied into a bundle. Since his wife died, his daughter has taken over the duties of an *istri,* a wife. She sprinkles water from a bucket to settle the dust, then to appease the demons, places banana-leaf offering of flowers and rice on the ground. She lights incense for the gods on the altar. Wayan waits.

The night hangs like a sling over Raye's little room. As the sunset fades, she resolves to make the trip into the village. She gathers up her satchel and sketchbook, and locks the door. From her treetop veranda she can see evening bats follow swallows, as they skim the last unharvested rice field. Neighbors at the villa are quarreling; the wife weeps, making low monotonous flute sounds. A sharp American voice carries, "What is your problem?" Raye feels sick in her stomach and sits down on the stairs. Raucous children in the alley play a teasing game, calling rudely to each other and running wild; their consumptive dog barks and hacks. In the pool, an Austrian traveler silently performs a froggy backstroke all alone. Suddenly all the misery in this fading world lives in her room. Now, she whispers to herself, I live alone. Stars wink on. The sky slips into something black. No moon yet.

A letter arrived that afternoon told Raye what she already knew. Her lover would not come to Bali. It was complicated, he could not explain, but he would not come now. Perhaps later, she had to be patient. They dreamed of Bali together. Now, she has Bali without the dream.

This is the most exotic place on Earth, she gushed in her first letter to him. *The air perfumed with frangipani, clove, and wood smoke. So strange and wonderful with primeval plants, wild monkeys, mangos, and papaya. I am writing this from my room at the villa. If I lean my head out the open window, I can see over the rice fields to the ocean, the placid Bali Sea. Today is fairly cool, and a delicious breeze is ruffling the palm fronds in front of my balcony. By the pool is a resting platform called a* bale *covered with bougainvillea. It has pink as well as white blossoms on the same vine. Yesterday, a woman on the beach offered me fruit – I could choose a dozen tiny bananas, a small pineapple, or passion fruit – for about the equivalent of 50 cents. Passion fruit looks like a mottled orange, but the skin is hard. When you break it open, out falls a glob of snot-like grayish stuff that surrounds the oval black seeds. It looks like fish-eye soup, smells like sweet pears, and tastes like perfume.*

Everything about Bali is as surprising as passion fruit: strange, unexpected, vividly colored, pungently scented. Behind the villa, a grove of coconuts and bananas; beyond that, mountains which fade into a blue haze in the evening.

Raye does not want to seem overawed, or unsophisticated, but she cannot help her infatuation with Bali. Seven months after their pledge to run away "to paradise" together, she sold everything, quit her job at the college, packed her paints, and booked passage to Denpasar. Three months later, going a bit slower, yet still living out of a suitcase, she waits for his call to say he is on his way.

Now, as the night gathers darkly along the path, she laughs. What a joke. It reminds her of a game her older brother and his friends played on her when they were kids. Hide-and-seek. You're it. Count slowly, one-one-thousand, two-one-thousand, three-one-thousand. . . and then they would be gone. Not hiding—gone. She laughs out loud. Yes, Raye tells herself, you certainly are It.

The path narrows and the stone wall on both sides turn into an abrupt alley. To the east the path opens up again to reveal the moon. Tonight it shines full, round, and vivid red-orange. The color of passion fruit. The village gamelan orchestra plays relentless percussive melodies with xylophone-like bongs and pings. Drums that sound like flutes follow her like a scent. She stops in the middle of the road sharply aware that she lives in a foreign land. She makes up her mind to stay in Bali. The gamelan hammers on into the night.

Wayan walks up the path from the beach to the villa. The path is dark, but his bare feet know the way. Six nights a week he comes to the villa to close the gate at 10 o'clock, and to open it again for any late night guests. Once, he had to kill a snake in a guest's room, but usually there is not much to do, so he sleeps in the *bale* by the pool so he can open the gate and keep an eye on things.

This night he closes the gate at 10 o'clock as usual, but must to open it again half an hour later for the American woman. She says "*Selamat malam*! Good evening!" with a strange accent. She looks directly at him, smiles. He repeats, "Selamat malam," but quickly looks away. Wayan goes back to the bale, his ears keenly tuned to the sounds of the night. He hears the rolling whirl of crickets, the drone of the neighbor's TV, the steady purr of motorcycles from the road, and the thumping of his own beating heart.

Raye locks her door and opens the curtains. The moon, now high in the sky, casts its cool blue glow from an unseen perch. Raye leans out the window to let the night wash over her. She cups her hands as if to catch the moon glow, then opens her fingers and lets the evanescence slip back into the night. She pulls the curtains shut and scans the room with a disapproving frown. Nearly three months at the villa and she still hasn't unpacked—ready to leave at a moment's notice. Now it is time to move in. She notices the letter on her desk. Raye traces his name on the envelope with her finger and brings it to her nose. No, she cannot smell any trace of her lover in the paper. She starts to take the letter out, changes her mind, tucks it back in, and hides the envelope under a book. She is pleased she does not cry. Completely weary, she lets down the mosquito netting around the big canopied bed and lies naked on the sheets. A gift in a box. But now she cannot remember who the gift is for.

Raye has been painting the rice field for over a month. Every day the color changes. The hour before sunset casts gold light on the field, turning the rice stalks almost transparent, shifting with blue-green shadows as they sway in the breeze. At the edge of the field, short stands of banana rustle their great drapes of green light in the gold dusk like silk banners. Her palette is a shimmer of transparent watercolors in Hooker's green, Windsor violet, lemon yellow, and aureolin, with occasional flashes of clear cool pink that mixes well to produce the shadow light she sees and can almost touch. The more she gazes at the field of rice, the more she understands the color is not green at all, but waves of alternating yellow and blue.

Raye notices that when grains appear on the rice stalks, the color becomes lighter but the plant heavier as it arcs toward the earth. Since the rice appeared, so have birds. Each morning and early evening as well, farmers come out to ward off potential thieves. One farmer, a man, arrives with his white silk flag on a slender bamboo pole. He waves the pole like a major in a marching band, whistling and twirling his flag to scare the birds. Another farmer, a woman, walks along the edge of her plot with a short bamboo sticks, which she taps together as she shouts, "Heh! Heh! Heh-*Yah!*" Organic pest control—Bali style.

Raye watches as harvesters from other fields arrive in groups of six or eight. They hide their knives, so as not to alarm the rice, and cut sheaves, which they balance on their heads and carry to the threshing tarp. In the field, they thrash the stalks as soon as they are cut. Empty stalks are bundled for another use, while the rice is bagged and carried on the heads of the workers. Raye wonders how people so small can carry such a weight, but they all do it, men and women, with practiced grace.

The setting sun stretches shadows and

floods the field with darkness. Outside her window, Raye can hear an old woman singing. It does not sound like Indonesia, it is a more ancient language. The cadence is like a prayer. The woman's voice meshes with other sounds in the night:: a dog's staccato barking; the steady drone of motorbikes from the national road; a pig squeals, its cry drawn out, long and low; the rusty-hinge sound of frog song; unseen laughter. A gecko punctures the stillness in between with a single note. The old woman's prayer-song weaves the sounds of the night into a symphony. If Ray could paint the old woman's voice it would be earth brown.

Trouble simmers at the Sand Bar in Kalibukbuk. By the time Raye arrives most of the boys have cleared out, except for her pal Stu, and Luther, a German wallpapered with tattoos. Luther hunches over the bar in with his bottle of beer, oblivious to the humid weather in his black leather vest. "What's up?" Raye asks as she steps over a broken chair. The manager, Putu, does not smile as he sweeps up broken glass.

Stu orders a beer for her without asking and lights a cigarette. Luther empties his bottle, nods curtly to them both, and attempts a dignified exit but stumbles on the curb. He revs up his motorbike, stalls, then finally kicks it into gear and roars down the street. Raye hopes there are no stray babies or cats in his path. Raye allows Stu a couple more puffs on his cigarette before fixing her gaze on him.

"Well?"

"Bloody stupid expats, nobody cares if they kill each other, that is until the *Touris Polisi* get wind of it, then there will be time and money to pay. This bloody South African comes in and starts bragging on his riches, his property, and all. Pretty soon it's all about women, don't you know." Stu motions to the waiter for another cold one. "Then the chap makes the fatal error of saying he fucked, excuse me, he *slept* with Luther's ex-wife."

"Oh-oh," Raye takes a drink, thinking of Luther's small head, big shoulders, and tattoos, thick black esoteric graphics that wound around his body from his ankles to his neck, yet not, so far anyway, onto his shaved head. A rocket about to go off, she thought at first glance. "Looks like he launched," she says aloud.

"What's that?" asks Stu.

"Nothing. Where's the other guy?"

"His mates took him off to get stitched-up."

Putu bangs the dustpan against the trash box and declares, "Luther not welcome here no more." Stu raises his glass in a salute, leans his elbows on the bar and gazes at Raye. He lights another cigarette and blows the smoke high, off to the side. "Oh bloody hell, I never met anyone like you."

"What do you mean?"

"You're so independent. You go where you want, do what you want. Don't give a rat's ass what people think."

"Sounds like you, don't you think?"

"Aye, we're two of a kind," he says with a wink.

"No, not really. Different species, actually."

"How do you figure?"

"Well, I'm a woman, you're a man, for one thing. And we belong to different continents for another."

"That's what I'm saying!" He is glad they are in agreement. "Aye, American women are something. They'll tell you straight away if they want you."

"Hmm," she says, looking out at the street.

"When I was in the States, that's how it was. They fancy you and tell you straight off. Had one woman, you know, we had a thing, then she wanted to introduce me to her Mum. When she walks out of the room, the Mum comes and sits down next to me. Wants me to talk, say something in 'Auzzie' just so she could hear me accent."

"Cute."

"Yeah, right. American women. Nothing like them." Stu takes a deep swig of beer.

"Except for American men. And Australian men," says Raye.

"How's that?

"We are the conquerors. First World. We're Number One! We have the money, the power, the bomb. We call the shots, quite literally." Raye's speech is a bit more vehement than she intends, but continues, speaks in a softer voice "That is why we can never really be friends with those we oppress. That's why I am not just little old me walking down the street, I am potential, I am money. We look at them as service, they look at us as payment."

"True, you can't trust the bloody bastards." .

"Well, we can't be trusted either."

"I've always been straight up. Done what I wanted. Fuck them all."

"Please don't do that."

"What?"

"Take your hand off my shoulder. Thanks."

"We could have an understanding," he says, trying to make his look meaningful.

"We do. I understand you are married."

"I do what I like."

"So do I. Besides, I have a lover. He's just not here right now." She swallows a sip of beer.

"Why is that?"

"He can't get away right now."

"Oh aye. I've always been one to make up my mind straight away," he says with contempt.

"Guess I am that way too."

"You should come round to the house. You could draw the garden. Paint the view," he offers.

"I would like that."

"Come round then."

"I will when your wife invites me." Raye smiles at his confusion.

"She won't mind."

"Not minding is not the same as being invited."

"Bloody hell, she'll do as I tell her!"

"Oh God." Raye sighs. " Look, I would like to come round to your place. I would like to meet your wife."

"Yeah, we each do our own thing. I've got my friends, she's got hers."

"Do you eat together?" Raye asks, suddenly curious.

"Eat?"

"When do you eat?"

"Late."

"Does your wife eat with you?" This is part of a social survey Raye has been conducting for years.

"Aye, she cooks for me." Stu doesn't like where this is heading.

"But you don't eat the same things?" Raye persists.

"She eats those bloody stinking fish with that Balinese spice. Turns your stomach, it does. Bangers and mash for me, mate. Veggies, too. Got to choke it down." He is tired of this talk, he wishes she would let up.

"You make it sound real fun," Raye says. They fall silent.

"Want another beer?" asks Stu, knowing her answer.

"No thanks. I've got be off." She tries to pay the bill, but Stu waves her off.

"See you later, mate."

"Aye, then." Stu shakes another cigarette from his pack.

Wayan steers his motorbike along the dusty path, not fast, not slow, as though his bike knows the way and he is merely along for the ride. The sun grazes the tip of the mountain, opening the day. He sees the American woman from the villa on the path. She too seems not to hurry, yet not going slow. She calls good morning. He slows his bike, asks where she is going, where has she been? Her Indonesian is getting easier to understand, or maybe he is getting used to her. He asks if she wants a lift. She says yes, and climbs on the back. At the end of the road he asks where she wants to go. Anywhere. Wayan heads his bike west, along the coast. They pass Seririt, just starting to wake up, the cart vendors wheeling their blue and green *warung* stands into their spots along the market plaza, past Brombong and Celukanbarwang—which you wouldn't even know were towns at first glance—on and on, past fields of rice and green beans, young cucumber, and yellow marigold. The landscape stretches out to open groves of tall coconut and sago palms and rows of banana between rolling hills. The Bali Sea comes into view, then is lost. On they travel, not speaking as they roll through the landscape.

Wayan stops at Puri Pulaki, where long ago an itinerant priest, Danghyang Nirantha, came with his family in the 16th century. The villagers asked him to make them invisible. This he did, along with the jungle full of tigers, where their descendents live today. Wayan tells her this story. She asks how can they know the tigers are invisible if no one can see them? Wayan shrugs. It is the belief, he says.

Monkeys at the temple gate follow them along the path. Raye removes her silver earrings and puts them in her pocket as a precaution. She has seen the thieves at work before. They climb the steep stairs to the top of the temple and look out over the sea crashing on the rocks, behaving unlike its sleepy self in Lovina. Wayan motions for her to follow as they continue along a narrow ridge past the temple up to a higher view. From this perch they have a panorama of the coast with the sea framed through temple carvings, monkeys acting as self-appointed sentries. Beyond the sea a faint outline of the island of Bali fading into the west.

They climb higher to a sheltered rock. Wayan rests in the shade, Raye sits beside him. Clouds gather around the sun. Then rain.

Persembahan — Offerings

Love Always

The sisters shared a teak armoire and chest of drawers, and slept side by side on their sleeping mats under a canopy of mosquito netting. Madé kept a photo of her boyfriend on top of the chest. Eyu, who had two suitors from the village, was yet undecided, so she kept their photos inside the drawer. A print of Saraswati, the Hindu goddess, graced the wall. The goddess of books, poetry, and creativity rendered vividly in Indian garb, with her arms, arms, arms, arms outstretched, held various accoutrements of her station: a *lontar* palm-leaf book; a *mala* of pearls; and a *veena,* a large sitar-like musical instrument, which the goddess held as lightly as if it were inflated with helium. Eyu, personally would have preferred Lakshimi, the goddess of wealth and beauty, in their room, but since Madé was older she got to choose. Even though the goddess of books looked over the room, there were no books in sight, only a portable CD player with Indonesian pop music disks scattered on the floor.

Although small, the room had a long, low window that opened to the west, with twining lilac clitoria and fragrant stephanotis. By the gate a small bush of white gardenia reflected moonlight on bright nights and exuded a sweet, spicy scent. But Eyu was rarely home at night to enjoy her father's garden now that she was a hostess at the Cinta Selalu restaurant.

Each girl had a basket on the chest that held her hair ornaments and combs. Madé had recently cut her long black hair to shoulder length, which caused it to spring up and back, like the wings of a flying Garuda. She enjoyed the effect and thought of herself as a modern Balinese woman, headed somewhere. Madé was studying to be a teacher in Singaraja and already worked part-time as a teacher's assistant mornings at a secondary school. Eyu kept her hair long, as her mother did, and grandmother, and countless other Balinese women before her. When undone it reached well past her shoulder blades. Straight, blue-black, it caught the light like a halo around her moon-shaped face. At work, she pulled her hair away from her face in a clasp. Her dark eyes turned up at the corners, set off by a snub nose, and lips naturally pink and full.

Balinese girls have straight backs and carry themselves upright, proud. As young girls they are taught to balance baskets of fruit, even furniture, on their heads. This cannot be done while slouching. Eyu had this natural grace in her posture. Her hands were long, with tapered fingers that she could bend in the manner of traditional *legong* dancers. That too, she learned when she was very small. She was still small, by Western measurements, petite, but shapely with a round bottom, tiny waist, and small upturned breasts.

At Cinta Selalu the girls wore traditional Balinese costumes for the evening shift—long, deep-red batik sarong skirts with lacy pink or coral see-though blouses worn with a wide satin sash. They helped each other to primp, tied their sashes tight, smoothed each other's hair. Each evening the girls would choose one perfect frangipani blossom to tuck behind her ear. They mirrored each other as they approved or adjusted with a glance.

Right after the bombs in Kuta for about two weeks the little village of Kalibukbuk was flooded with Western refugee tourists escaping from the south to bide time until they could book passage home, most back to Australia or Holland. After the initial flurry, the number of tourists dwindled until only resident expats remained: the gray-haired married Australian men, a lone German, an American painter who was by herself. And, one handsome young man on a long holiday from France, Michel, with his blond, curly hair, and deep violet-blue eyes. His penetrating gaze made Eyu's knees go wobbly. When he came into the restaurant Eyu forgot all about her two village boys.

Michel had business that took him to Singapore and Hong Kong, and had managed to parlay his annual holiday leave into the deal, which gave him two months in Bali. Part of his excuse for the trip to Indonesia was a textile project in Jakarta, but after two days in that congested nightmare, he approved the designs in progress and fled to Denpasar. He arrived the night of the bomb, but decided to stay anyway. When his frantic partner called asking him to come back to Paris immediately, Michel refused, saying he felt as safe as he would on the Metro. "Besides," he told Claude, "Bali has been prebombed now. It's not going to happen twice." Then he packed his bag and headed north to Kalibukbuk.

Each evening for a week Eyu brought Michel fried rice and Bin Tang beer, and made conversation in simple English that they both could manage. She leaned into his arm when she put the plate on the table. He never took his eyes off her. One evening Michel waited until she finished her shift at the restaurant and walked with her to her motorscooter, chatting until she started it up. Then, he leaned over the handlebars and kissed her sweetly on the lips. Eyu had been kissed before of course, but it had never stirred her like this. She floated home with the scorch of his kiss on her lips. That night she lay on the mat by her sister, her blood buzzing louder than the mosquitoes outside the net around her bed.

The next evening at closing, Michel waited for Eyu at the backdoor of Cinta Selalu again. He gazed at her with his violet-blue eyes and gently took her in his arms and kissed her slowly and thoroughly. Eyu nearly fainted. That night she lay awake next to her sister, her heart racing, her mind dizzy and confused, her lips still burning. Eyu was in love, of this she was certain.

Michel courted Eyu, sparking her with kisses and tales of a wide world beyond Bali. "Eyu, you would love Paris," he promised. Of course she would. She wasn't quite sure where Paris was, but it was not Kalibukbuk. Paris was bigger than anything she could imagine. Michel, entranced with his Balinese beauty, wanted more than just kisses, but she would not yield to him. She had been schooled against trifling sex; she would only trade her body, her gift, for a promise.

Michel took her to the Internet café and showed her pictures of Paris on the computer. The Eiffel Tower she recognized, but now she could see the Champs d'Elysee, great boulevards and gardens, the Louvre, and the Seine—a river that was walled, yet ran right through the great city—the underground Metro, outdoor cafés with tiny tables, boutiques, and beautiful stylish people, wearing overcoats in the rain. It all looked so strange and wonderful.

Eyu's village perched between the terraced mountain and the sea. All the houses in the village stood close together, separated by brick or stone walls, and overflowing gardens. Vines of purple bougainvillea bound one house to the next. Eyu's father kept their garden tidy with rows of planters holding specimens, starts and cuttings, and a pair of bonsai adenium with large pink flowers. Paint cans filled with green and fuchsia coleus were placed at even intervals along the top of the wall. The house was simple, low and shady, with cool white tile floors kept impeccably clean by her mother's twice daily mopping.

Eyu introduced Michel to her family, an awkward, formal meeting. First, he forgot to take his shoes off and tracked dirt onto her mother's white floor. He sat on the low futon couch and balanced the china cup with the plastic lid on his knee. He refused the sweets because he was a snob about such things and because he didn't think he could manage it with the tea. His refusal did not offend his hosts because he was a man and a Westerner. He didn't know enough Indonesian to really say anything to her parents and they only knew greetings in English, nothing in French. They sat while conversation shriveled in the heat. The ancient grandmother awoke from her nap in her chair, checked for her one tooth, then asked if the date for the wedding had been set? She asked the question in Balinese, although even in Indonesian, Michel would not have understood the words, but he noticed Eyu's blush and guessed the reason. Michel put the teacup on the floor, cleared his throat, and said, "Actually, *Pak, Ibu*, that is why I am here. I want to marry your daughter." Eyu was holding a tray of fruit that suddenly became very heavy. She swayed a little. Madé slipped her arm around her sister's waist. Eyu was stunned. She had no idea.

Michel hadn't either. He felt as if he were saying lines in a play. The rest happened in a blur, congratulations, more tea, and just like that they were engaged. The village priest was consulted, and decided the next new moon would be the happy day. The auspicious date was chosen, but had to be changed when Michel realized his visa would be up. An earlier auspicious day was selected. The ceremonial wheel began to turn. Michel paid for the priest, the food, and miles of *songket* fabric, as well as all the gold ornaments needed for the processional. Eyu's family and most of the village contributed elaborate offerings and many prayers.

Eyu responded to Michel's growing ardor with shy enthusiasm, becoming more pliant, meeting his demanding urgency with sweet passivity. He took her virginity two weeks before the wedding at his beach bungalow. She gave herself willingly and he took her gladly. He'd had many lovers before her, but Eyu was his first virgin and he was touched to see blood on the sheets. He vowed he would be a patient teacher in the art of love with his Balinese beauty.

Michel held his bride's hand as she submitted to the ritual tooth-filing, where her modest incisors were filed to be as even as the rest of her teeth. She said it did not hurt, but the procedure did not look comfortable. Michel let the family dress him up in the gaudy groom's costume, his torso tightly wrapped in *prada* cloth with a gold headdress, jewelry, songket sash, but he rebuffed the stagy eye make-up. And the tooth filing.

The wedding ceremony went on for nearly a week with feasts and visits from cousins and friends. The final day of the wedding began early in the morning and continued until long after dark. The village women transformed Eyu into a perfect little painted bride doll. Her long hair looped up and back in a complicated knot, held in place with crinkly gold leaves. Her pale face dusted with rice powder, her eyes fantastically outlined in black, her lips untouchable ruby red. Her large gold filigree earrings looked dangerously heavy. Her shoulders, like his, were bare, and her body wrapped in yards of glittering gold and red cloth. She held herself like a queen, with authority and grace. Her posture never faltered. Only once in the long evening did he see her stifle a yawn behind her delicate fingers.

In the family courtyard tables bearing offerings of fruit and flowers were stacked in tall pyramids; pinwheels and florets made from florescent-dyed rice created mandalas on the table. Opulent swards of red cloth stamped with gold encircled the family altar. The village gamelan orchestra pounded gongs and hammered out a rapid melody that rose and fell all evening. Everyone in the village came to see and congratulate the couple, and to eat the roast pork.

Michel could not wait to take Eyu back to Paris and show her off to his friends and family. He longed to unwrap his prize, but when the ceremony finished late that night, they were both too exhausted to make love. They collapsed in his little bungalow and slept for nearly a day.

After the wedding, the attentions of the family did not cease. He was part of a family collective now, his opinion sought, his vote counted on every issue from purchasing a new motorbike (to which he naturally should contribute) to procuring offerings for a village ceremony (to which he naturally should contribute).

At first, it was endearing to be part of this big, loving, nosey family. But he wasn't used to all the attention. He wanted to have his bride to himself, but there never seemed to be time for just the two of them, except late at night. At night he adored his darling and found she caught on readily to his proclivities, creative in her interpretations. He adored arousing her, enjoyed her pleasure as much as she did. Just having her in his bed to gaze upon excited his desire. Eyu was so perfectly made, so petite, yet voluptuous with the face of a girl and desires of a woman. He could not believe his good fortune that was triggered by a bomb.

They had been married almost a month when Michel's visa was up and he had to go back to Paris. Eyu would not be able to accompany him as planned. The Indonesian bureaucracy misplaced her application and her passport was not ready. He would have to go on ahead and make arrangements with immigration for her visa to France. He ruefully described his small bachelor apartment and promised they would find something better, a place more suitable for a married Frenchman and his beautiful Balinese wife. Michel looked forward to having her all to himself, so he could really love and pet her without all the little leering cousins and clucking aunties around. The constant company of her family did not seem to bother Eyu. She was comfortable with them and was ready to contribute a new baby to the fold right away, but Michel asked her to wait awhile. When it was time to go to the airport, Eyu, her mother and father, sister, grandmother, and two cousins insisted on going "for luck."

Michel kissed them all on both cheeks, said, "Adieu," as he walked up the stairs to international departures. Eyu, her mother, father, sister, and cousins wept. Grandmother wanted to know where the gamelan was that she could hear, but not see, and complained that the toilets were too tall to stand on.

Eyu went back to Cinta Selalu with a gold ring on her finger and an impatient yearning in her heart. She went back to sleeping next to her sister and dreamed of her French husband and mysterious Paris. She dreamed and waited.

Once in flight, Michel began to relax. Looking out the window at the green mountains of Bali growing fainter and smaller, Michel marveled at the island's perfection, now small as an exquisite blue-green jewel—as perfect as his Balinese bride. Back in Paris, his business demanded immediate attention. The textiles from Jakarta were splendid, but the Hong Kong shipment had been delayed. Singapore was calling. He had left himself little transition time and jumped right into the thick of it. Michel liked his work and had been gone for more than two months. It felt good to be back. Business was going well.

One week bled into the next until there were days when he forgot he was a married man. A month passed. Two months. He put off going to immigration for Eyu's visa. At first he was too busy, then, well, he forgot. Naturally, he did not have time to call his beloved Eyu and anyway her parents did not have a phone; he'd have to leave a message with a neighbor and call back later when she could be there. What was the time difference? Seven hours? Eight? He would see to that later, right now he had to catch up. Michel mentioned a holiday romance to his best friend Claude, but did not elaborate. He told no one about the marriage.

He reproached himself, then argued that the marriage, a little village ceremony, was not legally recognized. Perhaps this "marriage" was a silly indiscretion on his part. He wasn't really married, he reasoned, not in France. Eyu was just a beautiful Balinese girl he loved, but he had loved many women. He recalled how she looked at the wedding—a painted doll, so petite and perfect. Sure, he loved her, but a little village girl like that, how could she fit into a life in Paris? It was impossible. No, he needed to wait a bit and think it through.

Another two months passed. Michel's conscience pricked him, a little. Eyu was a lovely girl, but uneducated. She couldn't even speak French. Or English properly, for that matter. To take her from her village would be cruel. It was better this way, better to let go. Finally, he wrote the letter. It was brief, three lines in simple English. He said he was sorry, but he would not come for her. He enclosed an international cheque to be redeemed for three million rupiah. Enough to buy a young cow, he thought with a smile, recalling his little island paradise. Or a month's rent for a bungalow on the beach in Kalibukbuk. He posted the letter, shoved his hands into his overcoat, and went whistling down the boulevard.

Eyu waited patiently. She was different now that she was a married woman. Not so quick to giggle at silly jokes, not so breathless when the lace seller came with new goods. Her posture even straighter, her demeanor serene. She was a married woman who would soon fly to Paris to be with her husband. Eyu's beauty blossomed into full flower.

The letter took another month to reach Eyu. She read it carefully again and again, looking for some hidden code. She could not believe it. He did not even say he loved her. She lay sick on her mat, but did not cry at first. Eyu asked her sister, whose English was excellent, to read the letter. It was true. Michel would not come back for her. Eyu would not go to Paris. Then they both cried. They showed the letter to their mother and father, and finally consulted with the village priest. They held each other, they prayed. Then, they made a plan.

The next day, Eyu's father told the neighbors that poor Eyu's husband had been killed in a motorcycle accident in Paris. By the afternoon everyone in the village knew. Some said they were not surprised, they had seen him drive. The rumor held that Eyu's husband had left her a lot money. Eyu was a widow at the age of 20. She continued to wear her gold wedding ring, gazing at it sadly as she twirled it around her finger.

Then, one day she put the ring in the drawer with photos of her village boyfriends. She stopped mourning and went back to work at Cinta Selalu. Shortly after the festival of *Kuningan,* when the gods complete their sojourn on Earth and ascend back to heaven, Eyu said yes to Ketut, a boy from her village whom she had known all her life. She moved down the street into his family's house. A couple of months after the wedding, she was pregnant. There were two babies in quick succession. Ketut was well liked by her family and steady on the job as manger of a small sundries shop. He did not trouble her with burning kisses.

Michel still lived in Paris. Nowadays, he preferred to take holidays in the Canary Islands or on the Italian coast. Michel did not venture far from the continent. He sent his partner out on business trips to Asia. He had lovers; just one at the moment. She was married, it was difficult for them, they could only see each other occasionally. When they did manage it, they were content. She did not trouble him with burning kisses.

Ayam — Chickens

No Problem

Pak Agung felt agitated. There was no good reason for him not to be agitated, after all, it was the last week of Ramadan and he had been fasting from dawn to dusk for nearly a month now. But fasting wasn't what was making Agung irritable. Fasting, as he told his students, was *tidak apa apa*—no problem. Agung gazed out the open window of his room that faced the garden where a mango tree buzzed with flies. He polished his glasses on the end of his shirt. The pump still did not work in the pond. He needed to get it fixed. Surrounded by the comforting clutter of his desk and the teetering swell of books on the tiny bookshelf, Agung assured himself he was still in charge. He looked at the computer on the floor waiting to go to the repair shop. Another thing he needed to do.

His youngest daughter, Teda, entered the room on tiptoe, pirouetting and twirling, in a made-up dance, part improvised ballet, part Balinese legong dance. She carried a black plastic bag, which she held out to him. He reached inside and took out a stem with five or six rumbutan, a small red fruit with long, hair-like tendrils. Teda didn't have to ask; she waited until he peeled a few of the tough skinned fruits for her. "Now, don't eat too many," he cautioned. She stuffed two into her mouth and carried one, dripping in her hand. She skipped out of the room. Children weren't required to fast—God was merciful. Agung patted his own grumbling belly.

Agung smiled to himself. Both his daughters were sweet and smart, sure to grow into Balinese beauties. The girls had his wife's lighter skin and his black hair. Unlike his brother's sons, his girls would be fluent in English, the language of commerce. He would make sure of that. His brow furrowed again as his mind wandered back to his discontent. He could hear the television blaring in the other room. Both his wife and mother-in-law loved Indian soap operas. They followed the absurd stories with rapt attention, shrieked when the villain entered the bedroom of the beautiful princess, cheered when her lover arrived to vanquish the intruder. And the clothes the actresses wore!—or lack of clothes—withh belly buttons showing and all that gaudy jewelry: a ring in her nose, a ring in her navel, rings in her ears, rings everywhere. Indecent! But, Agung considered himself a modern Muslim man, he no longer lived in Java but in progressive Bali where people were tolerant. He was not a fanatic. He followed the rules of the Koran, he did not drink alcohol or eat pork, and felt himself above those who did. "To each his own." he would say benevolently. Tidak apa apa. "No problem."

He looked at his watch. His wife would be finishing her lunch and returning to work at the Singaraja Municipal Office in about ten minutes. She would be there until 5 o'clock. His eldest daughter would not be home until late afternoon. His mother-in-law could watch Teda until he got back. He waited until he heard his wife call out good-bye, and listened for the sound of her motorscooter as she pulled out of the driveway. He waited another few minutes, then asked his mother-in-law to keep an eye on Teda, reminded the child she must take her afternoon nap, put on his school jacket, and left the house.

The teacher's uniform was uncomfortable, the polyester clammy, but it made Agung feel more professional. It was, thank God, short-sleeved, a pale-gray Nehru-collar suit jacket with wide cuffed and creased pants. He tossed his old battered leather briefcase into the backseat of his Honda and drove away, as if he knew where he was going. He waved to his neighbor to the east, an old man riding a push-bike and nodded to the boy with the cart at the end of the lane selling chicken soup.

Agung drove out of town to the last stoplight and turned toward the sea. He was not sure why he was going in this direction. There were a lot of things he was not sure about now. He stopped at a new restaurant overlooking a rice field to the sea. A sward of cool green, a swatch of cool blue. He sat by himself under a canopy and ordered a Coke. He knew he would not drink it, but he needed an excuse to sit there. He stared out at the sea. A sudden gust of wind levitated plastic cups as utensils flew off tables. People lunged at their flying plates. One missed and frisbeed past him. He sat implacable with his soft drink and let the wind buffet him.

A white Kijang stopped abruptly in the middle of the road. Two women and one man got out of the car, shouting at each other. The man tried to pull one woman back into the vehicle, but she fought him off and kept walking down the road, her long hair whipping in the wind. The other woman carrying a baby, grabbed her arm. They struggled, but the long-haired woman broke free and stomped down the road. The woman with the baby screamed, then suddenly threw the child into the sea. People in the restaurant, watching the drama unfold, now suddenly jumped to their feet. A couple of men rushed to save the baby, but the man in the Kijang picked up the cast-off child. The potential heroes returned to their lunches, rather pleased that they did not have to get wet. The angry woman marched down the road toward the restaurant with the baby. The other woman got back into the car. The man slapped her a few times. Those in the restaurant either laughed or looked the other way. The couple in the car, the crying baby, the angry woman marching, all moved slowly past the restaurant as everyone turned their heads in unison to watch. Finally, the woman with the long hair got back into the car on her own, and the quarrelsome family continued on their way. The restaurant resumed its normal drone of clacking silverware on plastic plates, laughter rising and falling into the conversation. The wind died down.

Agung smiled at the waitress, "I guess that's the problem with having more than one wife." The waitress nodded, "Some people really can't afford it." This remark appeared to Agung to be incredibly astute. He paid for his untouched drink and left, driving up the coast, crossing over the path of recent dispute. It was the long way around, he knew. He drove on to Lovina and stopped at the villa of his American student, Raye.The Villa Aku, close to the beach, modern, nicely landscaped with flowering shrubs and a pool, was probably not more than two years old. Behind the stone wall, Raye's bungalow stood at the back, the upper story, with a clear view of the Bali Sea. Pak Agung was careful to address Raye formally as Ibu, careful to speak in Indonesian, slowly, simply. She seemed glad to see him and offered him papaya juice. Although very thirsty, he refused refreshment, as he was still fasting. She apologized. A pause. She looked up at him through her long fringe of blonde hair, her look quizzical, not impatient.

"Excuse me," said Agung, shifting into English, "I need to ask you something." She waited. "You see, something has come up, my nephew . . . that is my daughter," he faltered. "The thing is," he cleared his throat, "I need to borrow some money. I need a million rupiah. Can you help me out?" Raye flushed a little, frowned and put down her glass. "I'm sorry," she said without hesitation, "I cannot lend you money." She offered no explanation. "Tidak apa apa," Agung said quickly and shrugged. No problem. They exchanged a few more remarks.

He said he thought it would rain, she said she hoped so, she liked the rain, then they said good-bye.

He had another foreign student he could try. Agung drove to Jimmy's village. He didn't know where Jimmy got his money, but it wasn't earned, that much he could see. A nice young man, Australian, not educated, but smart, and Jimmy had a Balinese girlfriend. As Agung pulled into the driveway he could see Jimmy's motorscooter was not there. No, the maid at the door explained, Mr. Jimmy had gone to Thailand for a week. That surprised Agung . He didn't know there was that much money. Worse luck for him. Too late.

Agung raced back to Singaraja. He had nearly an hour before he should be home. He went directly to Ary's Jawa Warung, parked his car and crossed the street. The warung sold newspapers and sundries, tobacco and pints of American liquor. But the real business took place in the back, on the gaming mats. It started to rain. The roof had no gutter and water spilled onto the walkway. Pak Agung knocked twice, paused, then twice again. The door opened a crack, then seeing it was Agung, the doorman let him in. Ary, at a game in the corner of the room, did not look up. Two other games were in progress simultaneously. Small kerosene lamps provided a dim light. They exchanged pleasantries, then Ary asked, "Did you bring the money?" not looking at Agung.

"Look here," began Agung, "you know I'm good for it, I just can't raise it right now. School starts again in a week, I'll be able to pay you part of what I owe you before the end of the New Year, I promise."

Ary laid his cards face down on the mat. His dark eyes fastened on Agung. Then he smiled. "Ya, sure, tidak apa apa." Agung realized he had been holding his breath and began to let it out slowly. "No problem, my friend. But, the end of the year is a long way off. When you win here, you take my money right away. Now you lose, you must pay up. That is only right." He smiled almost sweetly. "Agung, I need that money by the end of Ramadan." He paused, lit a Marlboro, offered one to Agung who shook his head. "Sorry, I forget you don't smoke," said Ary. "Or drink," he smiled again. He took a long drag, nodded at Agung, clapped him on the shoulder twice, and resumed his game.

Pouring now, his head soaked, water ran down his neck by the time Pak Agung reached his car. He sat with the engine idling while windshield wipers slapped at the rain, and stared out at the dark afternoon. Rain filled the windshield, then the wipers cleared it away. Neither gave up—the constant windshield wipers, or the persistent rain. That God should appear to Agung between the rain and the wipers only slightly surprised him. Agung was a religious man, he believed in God and had expected to see Him one day. He had looked to the West, to his foreign students for help, but they could not save him. He had looked to the East, to his Muslim friend to help him, to give way. But he would not. At last God—God of all directions.

God called his name. Agung didn't know if he should reply, it seemed redundant to answer the All Knowing One. God seemed displeased. "Let me explain," Agung began. God raised His eyebrow. Agung knew the Divine was right, He was always right. God cleared his throat. Agung looked into the face of God. The face of the Divine was located between the strokes of the windshield wipers and the rain.

Agung tried again to explain. He illuminated his stellar qualities: he was a good father, faithful husband, giving teacher. He did not drink alcohol or eat pork. He tithed. Gave alms to the poor. He was planning a trip to Mecca, maybe in a year or two. Just this one little thing, one tiny vice: he could not resist the cards. Usually it was not a problem, tidak apa apa. Most of the time he was lucky. Just this once it got out of hand, he could not pay the debt. He beseeched his Maker and asked God what to do. God sighed.

Admit it, said God, *You are addicted to gambling.* Agung trembled. God sighed again and inspected at His cuticles. *This is not a problem to set forth before your Maker, Agung. This is just your confused little life. God is not in the details. I am not a micro-manager. You Muslims think the answer is in the* Koran, *Jews think it is in the* Torah, *Christians think it is in the* Bible, *and even here they disagree* – New Testament, Old Testament, *gold tablets or stone. The Hindus have the* Bhagavad Gita – *now that's a book I like, especially the part where Krishna shows the face of God to Arjuna."Stop! Stop! Don't show me anymore!"*

he says. Pretty funny. Ha-ha! But, I digress. Books are not the Word of God. I was misquoted. Don't you get it? I am not about Words. I am the Big Picture. I am not interested in you, per se. Abiding Love is a lot bigger than your gambling debt. Your transgressions bore me to tears. I have no answer for you, Agung. Only you have the answer to your problems.

As a good Muslim, Agung was taken aback by God's criticism of religion. Emboldened, he queried Him, "But why do you appear to me in the form of Man?"

This is your vision, replied God in a bored voice. *I do not have a form. I do not have a name. All of this,* he gestured at his cloak and beard, *is your illusion.* With a flick of the windshield wipers He was gone.

Agung, suddenly aware the afternoon had become quite dark, pointed his car in the direction of home. He left his shoes at the door and shook water from his hair. His daughters engrossed in a TV program did not even look up when he walked in. His wife called out, "Where have you been?" Agung went into the warm kitchen that hummed bright florescent light. "I've been talking to God," he replied. She went back to gathering napkins and utensils, brought out a cloth for the table, making preparations to break the fast. "Good," she said."Maybe you can make the prayer a little shorter this evening, since you've already had a chat." Agung ignored her blasphemy and kissed his wife quickly on the lips. Surprised, but pleased, she murmured, "What's got into you?" as she handed her daughter a stack of plates, then lit candles for the table.

The next morning broke clear and bright. Agung sat in his garden by the pond with the broken pump and surveyed his lot. God was right about words, he thought. Even though he loved words, he was good with words—Indonesian, Javanese, Balinese, English—they were inadequate. He looked at his garden, the swirl of greens and pinks and purple, all intent on growing, growing. They did not need words to communicate their intent. He peered closer into a hibiscus bush by the bench where he sat and saw ants and aphids, a salamander and a bright yellow bird he could not identify. Life supporting life, all of it intent, busy, like it was part of a plan. He wondered if God was going to visit him again. Agung waited. No. All alone, plus the insects, and birds, and lizards. This thought troubled him, so he put it aside and tried once again to find a solution to his problem in his wordless garden. Where was he going to find a million rupiah?

His gaze slipped along the garden path, traveled up the trellis and over the wall, traversing the big mango tree with its buzz of flies. He took in the ornamental carvings on the wall, the rock, the golden Buddha. The Buddha? He was a Muslim, his wife Hindu, that is, before she married him. What was a Buddha doing in the garden? He went over to the shady corner and parted the vines covering the small glinting statue. He picked it up. It was heavy and looked old. The gold color was not paint.

Ary counted out the money in 50,000 rupiah notes. Yes, it was all there, one million rupiah. "I knew I could count on you, Agung," he showed his teeth as he smiled. Agung nodded, relieved. "How about a game?"asked Ary indicating the gaming mat with his chin. "Go for two out of three?" Agung hesitated, then begged off. " Maybe later."

Ramadan ended with the celebration of Idul Friti. Pak Agung gathered up his wife and daughters to go across town to his older brother's house for the breaking of the fast. His mother-in-law, being Hindu, stayed behind. His older brother was the patriarch of the family now. The ceremony of forgiveness was first, and since he was younger, Agung bowed to his brother and asked for his forgiveness. Then his brother's sons did the same thing, each in turn. Then the girls. From eldest to youngest all asked to be forgiven. All were forgiven. All was forgiven. Tidak apa apa.

Kelapa di Bulan — Coconuts in Moonlight

One Coconut

A week of rain in Candidasa. Still the coconut men came for harvest. The ground in the coconut grove took the rain like a sponge. Only during a deluges did puddles and ponds form briefly—then a young duck family would sit in the puddles and dibble in the temporary marsh as they paddled in circles around the tall palms. Four brown ducks and one yellow. An odd duck, thought Raye, like me.

In the middle of the Bali rainy season the mature palms had sucked up so much moisture the coconuts were heavy. Raye had always thought it was milk sloshing around inside the coconut but the groundskeeper, Kedek, told her this was not so. It was coconut water, the milk extracted from fresh grated coconut. Raye examined the complex packaging. Before, she'd only seen coconuts as large, brown, hairy pods arranged in pyramids in American grocery stores, now she could see the true shape ovate, slightly pointed. The larger yellow, sometimes golden brown or green casing held a cellulose-like lining, another fibrous husk which cushioned the coconut's fall from the canopy fifty feet up or would help it to float if it fell into the ocean.

When the sun came out, the palms cast long leggy shadows the length of the grove. The sea winked and danced on the horizon in shades of blue gray. It was cool and quiet inside the grove except for the thump and splash of falling coconuts. The workers did not speak much. Each knew his job and set about it with practiced skill.

Raye tried to sketch the workers from her veranda. They were all so lithe, very brown, almost naked except for shorts or sarongs. A loop of rope fastened around their ankles gave them traction so they could quickly inch up the trunk of the palm by hugging it with their arms and feet. Once at the top they tethered themselves against the trunk to liberate dead fronds and knock down the ripe coconuts.

On the ground, other coconut men rounded up the nuts, some as big as soccer balls, and pierced the casing to string together in bunches of ten. A young man would then hoist a bunch on either side of a pole and carry them across his shoulders to the waiting pile. It was satisfying to watch the pile grow into a huge golden wall of variegated yellow greens and warm browns that Raye sketched and painted in watercolor. She took her sketchpad and stepped off the veranda into a gentle rain but did not notice at first that it was raining. She did notice little bumps emerging on her sketchpad, which registered as something odd with the paper, something inside the paper, not an external force. She was annoyed that the picture she was drawing was changing before her eyes. Someone said *"hujon"* and she recognized the Indonesian word for rain. It rained steadily as her vision shifted again. For a moment colors separated as color plates on a printer's press: cyan, magenta, yellow, black. A lizard on a tree that was invisible a moment before was illuminated in violet, his shadow yellow. Suddenly there were too many things to paint at once. Too much to see. Her mind went blank.

With more than two hundred coconut palms in the compound, it took the men three days to finish their work. They harvested nearly 1,600 young coconuts, stacked them high in the back of the Isuzu truck ready to take to the buyer in the next village, Sengkidu. Raye managed strong pencil sketches of the harvesters at work and was pleased with watercolor details of the coconuts, but had trouble arranging them into a satisfactory larger composition. She tried sketching a new layout when Kedek sat on the steps of her bungalow. Raye could see he was downhearted but waited a few moments, then inquired, *"Apa kabar?* How are you?"

"Not so good," he replied.

She knew Kedek well enough to wait, not to press him into a confession of his troubles. She also knew that sometimes he felt bombarded by her relentless questions, although he was generous and usually replied paitently. Because she was a Western woman she was privileged to share certain confidences that would seem unthinkable with a woman from his own village. Raye waited and watched the first spark of sunset ignite a corner of the sky.

Kedek saw Raye's gaze shift from his face to the horizon. He saw how her focus changed with the color of the sky. He often noticed her do this, how she disengaged with someone she was talking to and got lost in the landscape or an insect or a flower, as though these things were more important than anything a human being could offer. Yet, when she settled her blue eyes on his face, he felt she was the only one who could see him.

Horst owned the coconut grove that his hotel, the Kepala Kelapa, was nestled in. Married to Ida for thirty years with grown children—now grandchildren to show for it—Horst oversaw the entire operation. What people failed to understand he had other concerns. He was a very busy man. His furniture and antique business in Java took managing as well. But here it was impossible to get Indonesians to work properly. *Pilan, pilan,* slowly, slowly, they cautioned. Would Austria be a great nation if everyone took it so slow? Nothing would get accomplished. This bloody climate made them stupid. The workmen? They were boys, lazy boys, who would cheat him if they had the chance. Even his groundskeeper, Kedek, could not be trusted. He had employed Kedek and his wife for nearly twenty years, still he was certain if they had the chance they'd take anything that wasn't nailed to the floor. Horst intended to nail every bit to the floor or at least to oversee the process of nailing. The gall of it was they didn't even think of it as stealing; they just shared everything as though it belonged to everyone. Even though Kedek's wife was dead, nothing had changed. He was still a Balinese; what could you do?

Horst dreaded coconut harvest. He had to watch every one of the workers to make sure they didn't sit around smoking or talking together in Balinese, a language he'd never understood. Speak Indonesian! Of course his wife spoke Balinese, but he forbade his workers to speak it, although it was impossible to try to stop them when he wasn't around. He was a busy man, he had other business to attend to; he couldn't watch them every minute of every day. Horst could speak Indonesian well enough to be understood or misunderstood, as the workers fancied. He spoke fluent German and Dutch, as well as English, and a little French, enough to converse with his guests at the hotel. But Horst was weary of it all, the constant work to watch his workers every moment. He could never let up or it would be a disaster. They all wanted to cheat him at every turn. They stole fruit from the kitchen, took wood home for their own fires, wasted time. His repsonsibilities had no end.

Horst watched as a coconut harvester shimmied up the palm tree to the top. Even when he was a young man he could never have attempted such a feat. Damn monkeys. They were made for it, skinny little half-naked boys. All they needed were a few bananas and a cup of rice a day and away they went. He eyed his own naked belly. Substantial. Maybe a little too substantial but manly, he thought. He pulled in his stomach and stuck out his chest and strode across the grounds to the small pile of coconuts the boys were stringing together. "How many?" he demanded. The boy shrugged, as though to say, count for yourself. The other boy said nothing. Certainly easy enough to see there were five groups of ten strung together in a pile, but the insolence of the gesture infuriated Horst. These boys weren't his usual workers, they were outside hired help, otherwise he would have fired the boy on the spot. He scrutinized the canopy of palms and noticed where they had missed perfectly good coconuts or palm fronds that should have come down. He would send them back to finish the job. He glared up at the boy in the tree, his neck ached, his shoulder hurt; sweat trickled down his neck.

Horst yelled for Kedek. "When will they be finished?" he demanded. To Kedek this was a puzzling question. The workers would be finished when the work was done. Why did his boss need a particular time? They had been having this same discussion for years and always it ended the same. The work was done when it was done. Who could know more than that? "Soon," Kedek replied evenly. "Maybe this afternoon. Tomorrow we will go to Sengkidu." Horst seemed satisfied and went off to find a large cold beer and shade against the sun.

❧

Kedek hoisted another bundle of coconuts into the back of the truck, taking care to pack them in evenly and tightly. A good harvest this time and in another two months they would do it again. He sat back on his haunches as he waited for the next bunch to be delivered and looked out over the grove. He had planted twenty of the younger palms when he was a boy, when his family lived in a bungalow in the grove. Eight brothers and sisters: mat weavers, fishermen, farmers. It took many kinds of work to feed the family, just as it did now. Only now he did the work for Horst and Ida on land that was no longer his. Stay on, they had said to him. You can live here, and you and your wife can work for us. You know the land. We will help you with your children's education. But he never had a free day unless it was to go back to his village to help with a religious ceremony. The money was so small it was laughable; he was ashamed to say how small it was. True, Horst and Ida paid for uniforms and school expenses for his four children, but they deducted it from his salary, so he was always in debt to them. Three more years, he told himself. Three more years and his youngest son would be finished with mechanics school, then he would finish with Horst.

Ida was no better—a Brahman, the highest caste; why did she have to marry a European? She used the same tone of voice that he did. Always critical. Nothing was to their liking. They did not know how to speak, they barked. *Ini, itu, ini,* this, that, this. They made more work with all their talk, their complaints. Why couldn't they leave the harvest to the coconut men? What did an Austrian know about coconuts? A worker with another bundle of coconuts hefted a load into the truck. Kedek packed them in with the rest.

Kedek, up at sunrise the next morning, had the truck tarped and roped securely, ready to go. Horst had a second cup of coffee with his breakfast, checked his email, told the gardeners to cut back vines by the beach entrance and grumbled about the time. Kedek waited.

The trip to the village was delayed by traffic snarls and road construction but it was a short excursion, in spite of Horst's complaints and curses. What good did it do to say out loud what was obvious? thought Kedek. The traffic was bad. Did saying the traffic was bad make it better? Kedek kept his thoughts to himself but grew tired of Horst's endless complaints. If he wanted wide roads and fast cars why didn't Horst go back to Austria?

Kedek pulled up to the warehouse slowly and eased the truck into the dock where they offloaded the coconuts. Day workers were waiting. He chose a man his own age who long ago lived in his village. The man looked thin and worn. Kedek wondered about his family but didn't ask. The day grew warmer. They were both experienced and quick, but careful not to bang the coconuts or crack them open. It took less than half an hour to clear out the truck. Not bad. Kedek paid for his help. Then the man from his village asked for a young coconut. Kedek nodded and told him to take one.

Horst was busy in the morning, had to attend to business as usual, to give orders to his staff, and now the added burden of the trip to Sengkidu. His responsibilities never ended. He needed a break. Maybe he should visit his homeland and leave this impossible country, at least for awhile. When he was ready to go he called for Kedek and found him squatting in the dirt doing nothing. Finally, they got on the road, if that was the correct name for a potholed stretch of asphalt. No one in Indonesia knew how to drive properly. Either they went too fast or worse, too slow. Somehow they made it to the market and found some moron to help empty the truck. Horst turned away from the monotonous job to speak with another hotel owner. When he came back to the truck he saw Kedek handing out his coconuts—right in front of his nose! Stealing! He would not let this pass."What gives you the right to take my coconuts?" demanded Horst.

Kedek could feel his heat rising but fought against his emotions. He turned to his boss and asked "*Apa?* What? I give a man who is thirsty one young coconut. I think I have the right to do this."

Horst turned pink with rage. "You? You have the right? I own these coconuts. I hire you to work for me. These are my coconuts. You give away my coconuts to someone I don't even know. These are not yours to give, Kedek. You must understand me. It is the principle of the thing I want you to understand. Ownership. Mine. Not yours."

The man who held the young coconut put it back on the pile. Kedek looked away. Horst mistook the gesture for shame. It was shame, but shame that Horst had shown himself to the warehouse workers as a mean man, a man who would share nothing. Kedek waited for the anger to leave him. He did not want to move or to do anything when he felt this way. It was dangerous inside of him, a feeling of hatred and violence that he knew he must use all his power to calm. He did not want the workers to disrespect his boss, so he said nothing. Nothing.

On the way home, Horst shifted into another voice, that of a stern but kindly father. He instructed his groundsman, his charge. Kedek must be made to see how the world works. He needed to know these things, to not give everything away, like a Balinese. His children were practically grown and now he needed to grow up too. Kadek must understand that business is business.

The sun had slipped behind the ridge when Kedek finally sat on the steps of Raye's bungalow. She looked up and smiled at him, but he could tell she was still with her work as she frowned at drawings that were perfectly fine. At last she greeted him with "Apa kabar? How are you?" "Not so good," replied Kadek. "I almost quit my job today."

Raye put down her sketchbook and looked

at him full in the face. "Almost? Well, I'm glad you didn't." Kedek wanted to tell her the story of the one coconut. He hesitated, waited for her to ask what happened. But she did not ask, so he kept quiet. Raye looked over his head as the sunset colored the sea molten gold with delicate flicks of green and violet. A fine veil of rain misted the landscape. The rain created tiny prisms that seemed to magnify details of leaves and flowers, even the air in rainbow light. Raye took all this is in as naturally as breathing, inhaling and exhaling the beauty of the sunset, the rain, the sea. She smiled at Kadek and said, "You are so lucky to live here in paradise where most people will never even get to visit." Kedek smiled back and nodded, but did not follow her gaze. He did not look at the sea or the sky. He did not feel the rain.

Mimpi Ketut – Ketut's Dream

Two Wives

On Monday, Raj announced that Catherine and the children would be coming for the Christmas holidays. On Tuesday, the housekeeper cleared out evidence of the other wife from the bungalow. On Wednesday, Wife Number One arrived. Could Catherine smell evidence of the other woman in the bedspread or curtains of the airy little room? If she did, she kept her own counsel.

Catherine was the kind of woman one could describe as unflappable. Perhaps she had more English blue blood than Australian outlaw red. She had reserve and her wits about her. "It does little good to bang one's head against the wall," she would remark as though she invented the adage. She learned not to hear baying dogs at night or see trash along the path anymore, or to notice mysterious trucks that delivered teak logs to the villa late at night.

Catherine came to Bali once a year with the children. As Raj's wife she had certain privileges because she was a white woman from Australia and had red hair—attributes that were not in abundance in this part of the island. She was also the First Wife of Raj. What she did not know was an open secret in the village; the Second Wife, Wayan. Two wives are not uncommon in Indonesia, both Hindus and Muslims allow two wives. The Muslims say it is allowed if the man can afford it, the Hindus say it is allowed if the first wife agrees and the husband treats them equally. Raj could afford a second wife, but he was a Hindu.

Raj had many business interests that kept him in Bali most of the year. He owned the villa, bungalows, which he rented to tourists, the restaurant, teak smuggling, and a few other things neither wife knew about. Not bad for a barefoot boy who made his way from the north of Bali to swinging Kuta in the '70s to play piano at a hotel bar. That's where he first met Catherine. She was a real beauty then, with long red hair and skinny as bamboo. She really wasn't bad looking now, eighteen years later, but she didn't photograph well. Truth is, after Catherine had the children she stopped making an effort. She chopped her hair short, wore ugly owl-eyeglasses, and didn't give a hoot for clothes or makeup. She considered herself a sensible person. Raj wasn't around most of the time, and when he was, well, she certainly was not going to make an effort to attract him; she had stopped sleeping with him years ago. She wasn't about to start that nonsense again. Their marriage worked, she asserted, because they were both practical people. Gossips in the village might argue that the marriage was practical because they practically never saw each other.

Raj had his own version of their marriage that he would recite to English-speaking tourists who stayed at his villa and frequented his restaurant. "My wife and I don't get along," he would say with a sad look, "but she is a good mother to my children and that is the important thing." The sympathetic Australian or American tourist, usually a woman, would nod. "It is better that I provide for them," he would say heroically. Then he would name a sum, the amount he sent back to Australia every month for his wife and two kids. The sympathetic traveler would agree he was indeed a good provider. That was the deal. Back at the villa, the somnolent staff rallied to make ready for the official wife. Komang grumbled that it made more work for her.

"Don't you like Catherine?"asked Raye. "Oh yes," explained Komang, the housekeeper. "I like Raj's wife, but she always makes more work for me." Raye understood that meant extra laundry, folded and pressed—no tip.

That Raye was privileged to this insider information was an accident. By default of living at the villa long enough and chatty with the staff, she came to know a great many things that were best unsaid, but since she was an artist, not a writer, secrets were safe with her. She did notice that Raj's Balinese wife, Wayan, petite and sweet-natured, seemed more in scale with him. Sometimes in the evenings Raye would see them lying under the bamboo platform by the pool. Raj smoked cigarettes and spoke in a low, sonorous voice; she murmured back questioning coos, like a couple of doves.

Catherine was a good four inches taller than Raj, although with his expanding belly, he probably out-weighed her now. Their conversations did not have the melody of lovers' talk, it was all business, a staccato exchange that sounded more like a cash register. He could still be amazed at his first wife, though. Years ago, they were robbed in their home. The robbers used magic, scattered sleeping dust so that the whole family, including the baby, slept through the ransacking and theft of the bank bag with the night's take from the restaurant. "They didn't hurt us," Catherine said in her unflappable way. "All they took was money. We're fine." Raj didn't feel fine, he was shaken. It was Catherine, a Catholic by upbringing and nature, who suggested they bring in the village Hindu priest to bless the house and set things right again. After that they weren't bothered for a long time.

Yet Catherine refused to be a good Balinese wife in other ways. She resented the division of men and women at social occasions. More than once, at an all-day wedding she'd pay her respects, but after an hour or so get bored and demand the keys to the car, drive herself home. "What am I supposed to do?" Raj would protest. "Get someone to give you a lift," was her sensible reply. Raj understood he had married a Western woman, who was therefore exempt from the usual rules of a Balinese marriage, which is why he needed a second wife, a village wife—someone who would perform the duties that he did not have time for.

Wayan first worked at the restaurant, then he hired her to do the books at his woodshop. She had become indispensable in his business. Soon she was taking care of the flower offerings for the temple and participating in village ceremonies on his behalf. His sister first suggested the marriage. It made sense. He couldn't do it all alone. Wayan never argued with him, she treated him like a husband should be treated. Catherine was hardly ever here. He almost believed that if he had broached the subject of a two-wife arrangement with Catherine she would have seen how sensible it was. Still, she was a Catholic, so the subject went un-broached.

Raj's children were two average spoiled adolescents, but he was terribly sentimental about them, and thought they were brilliant beyond measure—perhaps because he paid for their private schools in Melbourne. They looked just like him with dark hair and skin just a shade lighter, but tall like their mother, with clipped boarding school accents. With his family at the villa, Raj had to show up, be the Dad, and sit with his wife in the evenings. They even ate dinner together. Still, they maintained separate bedrooms.

A week before Christmas, Catherine's parents arrived. Old Australian colonial-era in politics and manners, Mr. and Mrs. Sweeney were a pair of worn slippers, comfortable with each other and dependable. Now that Mr. Sweeney was nearly deaf, there were fewer things to argue about and they spent most of their time being amiable and uninterested. Even though it had been a good six months since they'd last seen each other, the kids were not motivated to get out of the pool to greet their grandparents and likewise the grandparents were more interested in a bracing cup of tea than embracing their future heirs. It was all very casual, congenial, and dull.

Their days took on the burnished patina of practiced ennui. The family collectively adopted a schedule that was as predictable as the afternoon rain—Raj would hurry away to work, while the others spent the morning by the pool, sometimes in it until tea. Afterwards, the adults played three-handed Hearts, and alternately praised and damned the rain, while the children waged war games on separate computers in separate rooms. Then, it would be time for dinner with Raj at the Sand Bar while the sunset painted the sea. They amused themselves with slight criticisms of what couldn't be bought in Bali, but were common in Australia. Mr. Sweeney would order a whiskey neat at dinner. Which would launch a new loquacious Mr. Sweeney, clearly absent when he was in the presence of women and children. Tonight, the subject was a favorite one: superior, intelligent, Western mind versus primitive, superstitious Indonesian mind. "If the Dutch had not come in, Bali would still be just an island of bananas and coconuts," declared Mr. Sweeney. "When I came here in 1968, the country was in ruins, poverty, crime, corruption. Say what you will about Suharto and his greedy family, but they brought the country up, gave people a chance at the middle-class dream. Now, it's all gone to shite again. The same six families run the show." He paused to take a long pull on his whiskey, thus refueled, began again, "This country has a bounty of riches, more than Australia could ever wish for." He cast a Calvinist eye on Raj, "But is it managed properly? Can anyone even do a bit of bloody business in this bloody country? Impossible! Maddening! Indonesians drive without their lights on to save electricity! They turn off their refrigerators at night for the same reason, and meat spoils!" Mr. Sweeney's blood pressure escalated. He ordered another drink.

Raj expected this part of the sermon; it was a familiar script. Although not usually a drinking man, he called for a beer anyway, and let a gentle beer buzz hum between his ears as he focused his eyes on the dimming sky with his attention far, far away. Mr. Sweeney droned on.

At last, Christmastime at the villa. An artificial Christmas tree, installed at the Sand Bar for tourists, played its own Christmas carols. The tree, strung with colored lights and plastic balls, had wrapped boxes beneath it that contained nothing and were for nobody. The kids were told the trip to Bali was a generous present and besides they didn't need to carry extra baggage back to Austrailia. Everyone in the family ordered what they fancied for

Christmas dinner and waited for their food while a recording of Jim Croce sang how he's got to get out of this place, he's so alone, New York is not his home. Meanwhile, *We Wish You a Merry Christmas* beeped electronically in time with the blinking tree, filling in silent patches between the dead folk singer's song and dinner conversation.

With Christmas officially over and the New Year a day away, Catherine was pleased at how well they were all soldiering through the holidays. She hated shopping, abhored the fuss and bother, or to be expected to do something, so Bali was the perfect escape from all of that. Raj spent extra time at the Sand Bar restaurant in an attempt to organize his staff for the big New Year's crowd.

The morning of New Year's Eve dawned sunny and bright. Cart vendors offered paper trumpets and silver-foil horns, fantastic noisemakers with frills of fluorescent paper and silver-and-gold fringe, and paper blowers with feathers to make a merry noise.

Raye sat at the Sand Bar in ritual observance of the sunset when the storms thundered in. One came tumbling down from the mountains, the other came rolling in with the tide. The crash of the two was bigger than any Fourth of July firecracker show she'd ever seen. One big crack from the sky and all the lights in town went out. A smell of ozone burned in the air. Sudden silence. A minute later an unbelievable amount of rain fell from the black sky. In ten minutes, the street was a dark rushing river carrying rocks, mud, and debris in a great swirling mass. Tourists at the Sand Bar congregated in the center of the restaurant as rain lashed through the open architecture and tried to drown the pretty floral centerpieces the waitresses spent the afternoon making. Small oil lamps quickly lit were brought out, but could not hold light against the wind. Raye walked up to the wraparound bar and ordered a beer. Raj sat alone in the corner drumming his fingers on the table. A portly German couple, copies of each other in male and female form, hunched together and doggedly perused the menu by flashlight. A middle-aged Australian woman and her young Balinese driver nursed their warming beers. The Sand Bar had enough waiters for each customer to have a personal attendant, but the staff clumped together while those at the tables did not speak. The storm raged on.

For two hours it poured. Of the half dozen people marooned at the restaurant only four bought dinner. The cart vendors with their paper noisemakers did their best to protect their wares under plastic, but it did no good. No one ventured into town. Around 9 o'clock, the rain downshifted into an average tropical shower, but did not stop until just before midnight. The electricity did not come back on until the next morning. The big party washed out. Those safe at home stayed there; those who came to town early gamely toughed it out. There were more boys in the band than customers in the restaurant.

Raye had a theory about New Year's Eve that one should be doing what one wanted to be doing in the next year. Some years that had meant making love, but most of the time she wanted to bring in the new year painting, making art. She had intended to watch the sunset and go home early that evening. Really, the last thing she wanted to do was sit at a bar, bored, not even drunk, not even interested, just waiting. At 10 o'clock, Raye surrendered to the night. She was in Bali, her first New Year's Eve in a foreign country. She would be a good sport, participate in a party with people she did not know, plus Raj with whom she could not claim friendship, and eight guys in a band that played pop tunes at least a decade old.

Around 11 o'clock, a Kijang pulled up with Catherine at the wheel. Raj was surprised she made the effort, but wasn't really glad to see her. Ten minutes later, Wayan made an unannounced appearance. Catherine sat at a table with Raj, but neither attempted conversation. He turned to the band and pretended to be lost in the music.

Raye knew both wives, but did not know if they knew each other. The idea of introductions, "Have you two wives met?" briefly crossed her mind, but she decided to be an observer rather than an instigator. She asked the bartender for a bottle of his best, now warm, champagne, from the bar lit by candles and oil lamps. The sea continued to slam the shore. Rain shifted into a drizzle, thunder and lightning played out.

Raye first waved to Catherine from her perch at the bar and offered her champagne. Catherine accepted a glass. Raye then waved at Wayan still hovering by the entrance and raised her glass. Wayan, now unsure about her bold move to be with her husband on New Year's Eve, waved back at Raye but did not move. Raye asked her to join them, to celebrate with a glass of champagne. "No," Wayan protested. "I don't drink." Raye feigned insult, cajoled her into sharing just one glass. It was almost midnight.

Catherine said, "Hello, Wayan. Fancy meeting you here." Wayan blushed. Catherine smiled."My word, you didn't think I knew? Well, of course. No, no one told me, but I knew that Raj had help, shall we say?" The women simultaneously turned to Raj. "Coward," muttered Catherine. Raye grabbed the bottle of champagne and an empty glass and said, "Come on! Let's all be friendly." The three women, a blonde, a brunette, and a redhead, marched over to Raj's dark corner. "Candles, please," commanded Catherine. Wayan said something in Balinese to Raj. He looked at once startled and chagrined. Raye poured the champagne. "To the New Year! *Selamat Tahun Baru!*" They drank as the New Year slipped in unnoticed.

Merah — Red

Asa

Asa came from Madura, a small island off the northeast coast of Java. She was a Muslim woman and therefore belonged to Islam, but she made it clear the religion did not belong to her. Raye, an American woman, did not call herself a Christian. Both women traveled under assumptions imposed on them by others. The two met at Villa Aku in the village of Kalibukbuk, kindred travelers, although for different reasons.

Raye had fled responsibility and boredom in the States. Mid-life crisis perhaps, a luxury only Westerners can afford. She quit her job teaching painting to untalented, spoiled, not-quite-adult college students, and packed up her art supplies in search of new inspiration. She settled, if that is the word for landing lightly, in Lovina, The Love Coast, an isolated part on the north of the exotic green paradise that is Bali. A single woman on The Love Coast—the irony did not escape her.

Asa, married, but had no children. She

smuggled teak which came from the national forests in Java. The intricate structure of corruption included pay-offs to everyone who could hold out a hand along the route from loggers to forestry officials, patrolmen on the roads and immigration police at the ports. They all had an investment in seeing that the teak made its way safely to Bali.

Asa traveled by ferry from Suraybaya ahead of the boat with the teak to customers waiting on the coast. The raw wood destined to be made into furniture or whittled into various bric-a-brac that eco-tourists would bring home from their two-week vacation. The great teak forest made small for a souvenir. It was Asa's job to see to it the money was in place for delivery and that the numbers added up. Most people think of smugglers as pirates, but it turns out they have many disguises, and the married Muslim woman disguise worked well for Asa.

The teak was always delivered at night. Lovina had the perfect bay in the Bali Sea—long and shallow, the water almost always calm. Raj, owner of the Villa Aku, would have his men load up the wood at night to take to his shop. The men constructed slings out of jute and hardwood poles to carry the logs that floated ashore to the waiting truck. Skinny guys, some of them barefoot, but all tough, well-muscled. Raye's impulse was to sketch the teak wranglers as they worked, but thought better of it. The teak business was an open secret in the village, but Raj still practiced discretion. No need to bribe more officials than necessary. Raj had other business interests as well as his guest hotel. His brother on the police force helped see to it that his interests were looked after.

Asa and Raye first met in the garden. The villa's office, practically part of the garden, was sheltered, but not enclosed, with no windows or doors In Bali, so much of the architecture is open and airy, opposite of the locked-up lifestyle Raye was used to. Guests could plug in their laptop computers and check email in the office or use the villa's one phone. Asa, in her long skirt and long-sleeved blouse, had her hair completely covered with a *hijab*. Raye, with short, choppy blonde hair, exposed arms, and little sundress, was her Western opposite. They looked at each other for a moment, then both smiled and exchanged greetings. Raye thought Asa absolutely gorgeous with her black almond eyes, smooth brown skin, and dimpled smile. She appeared to like Raye as well, fingering her blonde hair like it was silk. *"Cantik,"* she whispered. Beautiful. They were mutually enchanted to find each other. Two sides of the same coin. Asa told Raye she did not know exactly how old she was. She was probably ten years younger than Raye, but it was hard to tell. Raye was fifty and had a cultivated attractiveness. Asa was simply a natural beauty.

Later that evening, as the sun was sinking into the bay, turning the rice field that surrounded the villa into green-gold, Raye saw Asa in the garden, in her long, colorful garb and her shining, golden face. Raye grabbed her camera and ran down the steps of her bungalow. She wasn't sure what the Muslim rules were about photographs, but Asa said yes. Raye felt an urgency to capture the golden glow of her new friend. Most Balinese people are happy to oblige with a smile when you point a camera their way. *"Boleh, saya foto anda?* May I take your photo?" Raye asked. Asa smiled, pleased to be asked. Or maybe she was smiling at Raye's odd Indonesian pronunciation. Asa posed sitting by the pool, but Raye had another idea, and placed her in front of pink bougainvillea, and again by yellow hibiscus. Later, when she showed Asa the photographs on her computer, Asa modestly agreed that she did look lovely. Raye admired her candor.

Asa had waited for three days. The teak delivery was late. Each evening, she would disappear behind the office to do her *mandi*, to bathe in the tiny bathroom back there. Raye knew the ritual was to disrobe and stand before the tiled cistern full of clean, cool water. With a plastic scoop you splashed the water over your head, soaped your body, and rinsed again. After the mandi, Asa would change into her other set of clothes. Raye admired how cool she always seemed to be. "Look at me," she demanded. "I'm wearing practically nothing and sweating like all get out, while you are cool as a cuke under all those blankets." Asa didn't quite understand what she was saying, but always smiled when Raye attempted conversation. Asa spoke some English, but not that well. Fluent in several Javanese dialects, and Indonesian, of course, and she liked Dutch and could even speak some French.

That English was a bit lower on her list of linguistic talents selfishly disappointed Raye, whose Indonesian was primitive, but they did remarkably well with what few words they shared.

The next evening at sunset they ran into each other at the villa's gate. Raye on her way to the village for dinner, Asa had just come back from the beach where she had picked a large, pale-green fruit, which looked like a small squash. "What is that?" Raye asked in her in Indonesian. Asa told her the name in Javanese, but Raye couldn't get her mouth to repeat the unfamiliar combination of sounds. Later, she found out it was a type of passion fruit. She regretted she had missed a chance to invite Asa to dinner.

Jean, a Dutch salesman who lived downstairs, told Raye he met another smuggler with his handlers last year around this time. "They just wait for the teak, then they wait until the money comes. Madura is a very poor island, rocky, not much there. They are a fierce people, willing to take chances. They have a rigid code of honor. No one cheats someone from Madura. When they come here and have to wait, they must rely on others to feed them. With nothing to lose, what else can they do?"

Raye overheard Asa speaking on her cell phone to someone. Who? The boatman or another smuggler, perhaps? Her manner was quite forceful, she spoke rapidly, without giving in to any argument. It was clear Asa gave the orders. The next day, a boat toting the barge with teak anchored off the bay. In the evening the logs floated ashore with the tide and help from the men who pulled them in.

One morning, Asa glanced up at Raye's balcony and saw her stretching into yoga. Asa looked away and walked on. Asa once remarked that American women had no shame. That's how Komang, the housekeeper, translated it. "You have no shame." Not like she ought to have shame, but rather had simply arrived without it. Asa did not judge Raye, she simply stated her observation.

They had wonderful, slowly translated conversations between Komang, who knew more English than Asa, and Raye, whose Indonesian was elementary. In her culture, Asa had always been told that her body must be covered. If a man looked at her with bad intentions, it was because she had led him to bad thoughts.

Asa did not feel shame for her body. She silently rebelled against that idea and took secret pride in its strength and beauty. They talked about sex. She knew how to prevent babies, but her husband did not know she had this knowledge. Her husband took his rough pleasure with her, and she took pleasure in their lovemaking as well. This made her laugh and laugh, a great joke on him. As a modern Muslim woman, Asa was careful about the rules. Her husband expected her help in the family business selling teak. She never failed. She knew what others expected of her, yet she also took care of herself.

Asa saw Raye as an American woman unconcerned about what others thought. She presumed she must be very rich, and of course, by Indonesian standards and the American dollar exchange rate, she was. With no husband, no rings, only silver bracelets on both arms, Raye could walk where she wanted to, and go out at night. Sometimes, Raye would drink a beer with a married or unmarried man. Asa also noticed that her new friend spent a lot of time alone in her room painting and drawing. "Passing time," remarked Asa, with a wry smile, which irked Raye a little.

Both women could wait; they had that in common. Raye waited each day for the early morning light and, at dusk, when she could paint and get the colors just right. Asa waited for the boat and the money. Raye sometimes waited by reading or writing letters. But Asa could wait by simply waiting. They admired each other's patience.

That Saturday evening in mid-October passed as it usually did. The night was particularly quiet in Kalibukbuk, even the dogs were unmotivated to complain. The moon shone like a golden cat's eye in the black sky. The news of the bomb in Kuta spread fast. Raye heard first through an email contact in California. Thirty, no, eighty, no, a hundred. More than two hundred people, dead in the nightclub blast, mostly Indonesians and Australian tourists. Militant Islamic terrorists were suspected. A story so common, it was cliché. Everyone at the villa knew someone who might have been in Kuta at that moment. Another kind of waiting now, a terrible waiting. They could do nothing more.

The day passed and night came on suddenly. Raye stepped out on her balcony to look at the emerging stars, fixing herself on the map in the sky. Down in the garden, Asa was doing the same thing. Raye waved. Asa waved back. "Come up, see the stars from up here. It is closer!" called Raye. Asa did not hesitate. From the balcony they could see the Bali Sea silhouetted by a fringe of coconut palms with a faint outline of the tip of the island on the horizon. Venus burned steadily in the sky. The mother-of-pearl sea held the moon as gently as a spoon. Raye reached for Asa's hand, their fingertips brushed slightly, then clasped together. The night, now suddenly still, exhaled the fragrance of frangipani. The moon hid behind a palm.

Setelah Hujan — After Rain

Uncle

The American built his house according to the principals of Tri Loka, the Hindu idea of dharma, and the division of the universe into three realms — the realm of gods, realm of humans, and realm of demons. All had equal weight. Each must be aknowledged and honored.

The house was near the beach. It was built in the grand Balinese style, with a lavish garden and large family altar. There was even an eleven-tiered meru for Siwa, the most important god. Slowly and carefully Uncle laid out his estate, consulting with local experts on the physical as well as spiritual implications in the design and placement of every detail. The garden was a wonder, filled with mangos, papayas, coconut, and banana trees, as well as three kinds of sweet-smelling frangipani. Some exquisite flower was always in bloom. If you happened to pass by on your way to the beach, spicy, alluring fragrances wafted over the wall, which made you slow your step and linger a little as you passed Uncle's gate.

The American built slowly and carefully, the first season the house, the next the garden and altar, then the pool. The blue-tiled pool had a long slow incline, so if you were a child or short, you could stand in far end, but if you wanted to really swim it was long enough for laps. It was all very well-thought out. The house too, although it looked like the traditional Balinese house, with a clay-tiled roof and narrow, carved wooden front door, was actually quite modern with Western-style plumbing, and a unique cooling system that fanned air through the house without icy air conditioning. Subsequent seasons Uncle was able to enlarge his compound by buying property to the west and east. Here he built the guesthouse, sketched after a Balinese rice barn, and a playhouse, a long, low pavilion with a few small enclosed rooms off the center. The main house, guesthouse, pavilion, and pool were linked by a series of intimate courtyards.

Everyone in the *banyar,* the village, was proud of the American's house. In fact, many people in the village had a hand in building it, or planting the garden, or installing the pool. In the village he was called simply *Paman* or Uncle. He was known to be both generous and fair. He was generous to children, too, particularly little boys. The play pavilion had been built specifically with them in mind. Paman had all sorts of nice playthings: electronic gadgets, video CDs, a PlayStation, and other games. His cook made lovely things to eat for snacks, like toasted peanuts, coconut cake, and cold Coca Cola to drink. You were a lucky boy if Paman asked you to his house. Sometimes you could be invited if another boy asked Paman and he said it was okay. Sometimes Paman met new friends at the beach. He always made sure it was all right with their parents for them to come over after school. It was only for a couple of hours.

The boys would play in the pavilion or swim in the pool and have their snack, then one boy would be chosen to go into the private room with Paman. Later, when that boy went home, he could take a fifty-thousand rupiah note to his mother, more than she could make from a week's worth of laundry.

Gede longed to be invited to Paman's house. His cousin Wayan got to go on Wednesdays and told Gede about all the wonderful toys in the play pavilion and the swimming pool, and the cold Coca-Colas. It was a special place and only special boys could go there, he explained. Gede wanted to taste the coconut cake Wayan described and to try out the PlayStation. Wayan had been chosen by Paman one day when he was with some friends at the beach. Paman was very nice to all the boys and bought them ice cream from a vendor and later told Wayan to ask his mother if it was okay to come to his house on Wednesday.

Gede went to the beach everyday and waited for Paman, but Uncle did not come to the beach for two weeks. One day, Gede was sitting on the shore drawing in the sand with a stick when one of the other boys saw him first. "Paman! Uncle!" The boys shouted and ran to him. Gede was shy at first, but lined up to get his ice cream with the others. Paman did not invite him to come to his house on Wednesday. But the ice cream was still good.

Another week passed. Then Paman came to the beach again, and this time he did invite Gede. He asked his mother if it was okay to go to Paman's house on Thursday. Yes, of course, she said, it would be an honor. The play pavilion was just as Wayan described it. There were lots of electronic toys, interesting things he had only seen before on TV. Gede played with the other boys and got to taste the coconut cake. For three Thursdays in a row, Gede went to Paman's house. On the fourth Thursday, Paman asked Gede to come with him into the private room. The boys didn't talk much among themselves about what went on in the private room. The first time was the most difficult. Then they got used to it. It was normal. Paman didn't hurt the boys, he just wanted them to do special tasks for him, sometimes with their small hands, sometimes with their little mouths.

Some of the boys, when they got older said they even liked doing what he asked of them. But when you got older you couldn't come back to Paman's place. Only little boys were chosen. All this Gede learned in the year that he was privileged to be invited to Uncle's house.

The parents, of course, knew about Paman's special requests. They were pragmatic. If Paman would help to pay for the school uniform, give them a few thousand rupiah, then they were lucky if their son was chosen. He got to play electronic games and watch TV, and had nice things to eat. And the money helped the whole family. The things he had to do in the private room, well, that was just part of the Tri Loka. One must respect the demons as much as the gods.

Wayang Kulit—Shadow Puppets

Too Good for Ubud

Clive sat on his veranda with his gin and tonic, and gazed out over the rice fields. The setting sun mirrored in the still water of the fields and in the curving steps traced contours of the green mountain that reflected a lemon-yellow sky. That color was the perfect shade for the walls in the Borge's new bungalow, he thought. What would he call it? Sunset-yellow? No. That would imply too much orange. Lemon-yellow too ordinary. *Kuning?* Yes, the Indonesian word for yellow—kuning. Light but regal. It sounded like coin. Kuning, the perfect color for the walls. He would say, Clarissa, we need to warm these walls with a gentle wash of kuning. And she would clap her hands and say, Oh, Clive, you are brilliant! Kuning! Of course! Let's have drinks to celebrate.

It was amazing how easy it was here in Bali. Of course, Clive had always been successful, when was he not? But in Amsterdam he'd decorated houses of government ministers and pop stars, and never knew when they'd come through with the money. Rich people were often careless that way. Here, in the tony enclave of Ubud, rich expatriates clamored for his services, which were strictly pay-as-you-go. His interior design work had been featured in the best glossies. Balinese textiles and carvings, so much of the art exquisite and so lovely to work with. Cheap, my God! It was cheap to buy things here. How satisfying to design without budget worries. Hard to remember he was in a Third World country. Emerging Country, he reminded himself. Emerging World.

He scanned the living room of his own bungalow with a critical eye. Magnificent, he had to agree with himself, a real showcase for his talents. One of his talents was entertaining, bringing together the best and brightest. He smiled at that. Okay, maybe just the richest and most connected. Nevertheless, that counts, he reminded himself. Definitely counts. He glanced through the open carved doors at the casual arrangement of poufs and pillows, the rich assortment of songket cloth shot through with silver and gold. And ikat weavings, in his made-to-order colors, slightly out-of-focus designs, in misty shades of green, violet, and gold. He scrutinized the pale eggshell walls in his living room. Maybe they could use a wash of kuning as well.

Clive finished his drink, slightly annoyed that his new houseboy was not there to refill it. This mild displeasure barely had time to register as a crease on his forehead, when Gede glided into the room with a fresh drink. Rather than pleased, Clive grew annoyed at the presumptuousness of the gesture. "I didn't say I wanted another drink," he said, a little more petulantly than he meant to, as he took the glass from the lacquered tray.

"Ma'af," apologized Gede, removing the empty glass as he lowered his eyes. Beautiful eyelashes thought Clive, watching the young man move with the grace of a dancer through the room. Gede was well formed, his skin tawny with thankfully no visible tattoos. Black hair, a little longer in the back and shiny, like a pelt. Clive watched his servant leave the room with an aesthetic satisfaction, as one who has happily made a handsome purchase.

He knew he should go to his studio now and draw up some ideas for the bungalow. Easy work. Still, it had to be done. He must demonstrate his talent went beyond just talk and shop. The drawings were important—it gave the client something to show her friends—it showed off his pretty hand at illustration. His hesitation had more to do with lack of interest than true laziness. Actually, he could probably go to his files and pull out an illustration completed three years ago and pass it off as the latest brilliance of Clive Dearborne, Inc. Truth be told, he was bored. The seeming friendships with these dowagers, or recent divorcées, or gay businessmen were all so predictable. What was it he read in *Vogue*? That a gay friend was as essential as the cocktail dress. And a gay interior designer? Darling, he was the new black! It got tiresome. Clive noticed with regret his second gin and tonic stood empty.

He tried again to rally interest in the project. He suddenly realized brightly that Clarissa was neither a dowager nor divorcée, just simply a thin, long-haired blonde with a generous German husband, who thankfully was very much involved with his work. Something to do with Mercedes. A Mercedes guy, she said. He doubted Clarissa even knew what her husband did. No matter. This sketch mattered. First, answer the question: What is the goal of this room? He rehearsed the conversation he would have with Clarissa. He would instruct her; she liked that. He would say, "Clarissa, the purpose of this room is to seduce. In this room you shall arrange yourself on cushions, or drape yourself over the divan. This is a room for posing and play, for seduction and love." He would demonstrate a few poses and she would laugh. Although he suspected she liked the idea of posing and seduction more that actually making love. She seemed much too contained to overtly loll about on cushions and show off those long, slender legs. For one thing she did not eat. As far as he could see, she did not consume solid food, although she liked to drink well enough. Clive noticed that women who did not like to eat, also did not like to fuck.

We are dealing with the living room, Clive reminded himself. The space not all that big, but the architect had cleverly contrived to make it feel spacious. He hoped the new house would weather the rainy season. Often there was a discrepancy between design aesthetics and practicality in the tropics, one of the many reasons he was glad he had switched from architecture to interior design in school. The bones were someone else's problem. He was all about skin. An idea for animal hides: leopard maybe, mixed with Balinese weavings. No, too overtly primitive. Clarissa would be too PC for that. Besides, one must not mix too many metaphors and the Balinese aesthetic was sophisticated enough. Anyway, that's what he would say. Perhaps he could persuade Clarissa to do something innova tive with glass, something different with lighting.

Riding on his gin and tonic high, and inspired with ideas for color and light, Clive finally began to draw. He laid down basic ideas in colored pencil, then snazzed it up with a watercolor wash. He was one of the few designers around who did not create his presentations on a computer. The drawings gave the impression of being unique. It wasn't difficult, Clive mused a little bitterly. His clients were always impressed with his handsome illustrations. Yes. He did have the touch.

In the bright morning light Clarissa squinted at the pretty rendering. Clive realized he made an tacticle error scheduling a morning meeting. Too early in for drinks, but not too early for the teensy-weensy hangover Madam was trying her best to set upright. "Clive, I absolutely adore this drawing," she began, "but I don't know about the yellow walls." "Kuning," interjected Clive, irritated that his timing was off. "Not really yellow, a hint, a wash of lemon, " he insisted. "Kuning."

"I'm not convinced," Clarissa said firmly, and Clive saw at that moment she was more savvy than he'd given her credit for. Of course, yellow would not be enough contrast for her pale beauty. With yellow walls, kuning, whatever, she would blend in, not stand out. Yellow was not the right backdrop for her stage setting. It would have to be rose-pink or sea-blue, like her eyes. Clive surrendered. "I see what you mean."

Clarissa splayed her long fingers out on the table, framing the drawing with her pearly manicure and gold rings. "I just love working with you Clive," she purred. "And the songket cloth is divine." "Of course." He lobbed one back into her court,. "It sparkles just like you do, Clarissa." They were girlfriends again. Now they would shop.

After a full day with Clarissa, shopping in tiny mountain villages for hand weavings and split bamboo furniture, Clive thought he'd enjoy a nightcap with the boys at Café Luna. Cisco and Dion always had the latest gossip from Lovina, and Dion in particular knew how to dish it, but Clive felt strangely not in the mood after half an hour. He wanted to hurry home to the calm of his own bungalow and his really good sound system. He wondered what Gede, his houseboy, was doing. He hummed as he pulled the car up the narrow dirt road to his house.

Gede had arranged frangipani blossoms along each step to the veranda. He approached silently on bare feet, opened the door and inquired softly if Clive would like a drink. Sweet sandalwood incense wafted through the hall. "No. No, thanks. The place looks great, Gede." The young man looked pleased at the mild praise. Clive stared at the lovely way Gede's collarbone shone in the moonlight. He allowed his gaze to hold on the adorable sweep of eyelashes for just a moment before reasserting himself as master of the house. "Would you draw me a bath, please." "Certainly, sir." There. They were back in their proper places. Gede, naked to the waist, his slim hips wrapped tightly in a batik sarong, turned to the task.

Alone in his bed, he kicked off the finely woven Egyptian cotton sheets. Clive allowed his imagination to wander over the unknown terrain of his houseboy's physique. He gave his own hands free access to his overheated body, then cancelled the invitation. Self-sex was not wat he wanted. He dreamed of Gede's fluttering eyelashes.

Clive awoke to the scritchy sound of a palm broom sweeping the garden path. He looked out his bedroom window to see his houseboy at work. One hand held the bundle of sticks, the other hand, palm up, rested lightly in the small of his back as he leaned into his task. Gede had already swept away the debris and now used the broom as an artist would use a large brush to leave a calligraphic cipher in the loose dirt, inscribing half circles as he walked backward along the path. The early morning light glanced off his naked shoulders, emphasizing the contours of his back. Clive began to whistle softly. What a find, what a delight, he thought, pleased at his good luck.

Fresh brewed tea waited to be poured. Gede had set the Chinese celadon teapot and cup outside by Clive's favorite chair in the garden and garnished the arrangement with a perfect crimson hibiscus blossom. Wrapped in a short cotton kimono, Clive sipped the tea and mused how he would like to dress Gede as a male version of a geisha in a kimono much like his own. Maybe a bit shorter. Or as a sultan's bodyguard, bare-chested with ballon pants and a scarlet sash with a dagger. Or maybe as a French maid. No, that was going too far. In a holiday mood and restless, Clive called out, "Gede, I want to go to Lovina and would like you to drive. Please bring the Kijang around."

It was only a two-hour trip, but the road curved along steep ravines, through the mists of Bedugul and up, up the mountain through clove-scented air and jungle thick with coffee bushes and jackfruit trees. At last a roller-coaster ride through Gitgit into Singaraja, then the long flat horizon of the Bali

Sea. Ubud often seemed confining to Clive after a visit to Lovina, the steep mountain town and the flat coastal village in sharp contrast. Gede made the drive seem effortless, deftly dodging motorcycles and overtaking bloated trucks along the narrow road with a light touch on the steering wheel and steady pressure on the accelerator.

Clive headed straight for the Sand Bar, where he saw Cisco and Dion already holding court. "Hullo, mates!" Clive called out in a mock-Australian accent. Dion squealed and Cisco smiled and waved. "How did you guys get here so quickly?" Clive wanted to know. Dion looked coy, but Cisco explained, "We drove in last night. Ubud was totally dead, but Dion was still up for some fun so we drove to Singaraja where we caught the last act at The Temple. Lil' Lakshimi was performing."

Dion nodded. "She was good," he admitted, "but I have a lovelier figure." Dion's brag was true and all the boys at the bar knew it. Dion waved at Gede waiting in the car. "What enchanting ornament are you keeping from us now?" he demanded. Clive tried to halt the blush that singed his cheeks, but his friends could tell instantly he had more than a professional interest in his driver. "My new houseboy," he said. Dion let out a whistle of appreciation. "He is rather pretty, don't you think?" Clive tried to sound casual. "More than rather," gushed Dion. Clive intercepted his thought. "No, you may not invite him to drink with us. I need someone sober with me tonight." Dion stuck out his lower lip in a pretend pout, but let it go.

They agreed to stay at Villa Aku and decided to rest up in preparation for the night's drinking by checking in early and lounging about the pool. At the villa, Clive sent Gede on a nearly impossible task to find potted purple orchids in Singaraja. He did not want to be distracted by his houseboy's beauty this afternoon; he needed time out. Cisco and Dion were still fussing with their Speedos in their room. At the pool, Clive recognized a couple of American expats he'd encountered before in Lovina. Two brothers, brown as baked potatoes, sat on the stairs in the shallow end of the pool with cans of Diet Coke in one hand, Lucky Strikes in the other. Too early for a Bintang—they weren't alcoholics. They would wait until noon to start drinking. Mirror images of each other in corpulence and color, except Garth, the younger one, had a shaved pate, while Rocky, the elder, kept his mouse-gray, curly locks long and unruly. They argued as easily as breathing, settling into a dispute over the correct address of a house they had lived at some forty years ago, when the blonde woman slid past them into the pool. The late morning was hot and getting hotter, but she was cool and remote, swimming with long, even strokes, paying no attention to their argument bubbling at the other end of the pool. Clive nodded to the troglodyte brothers as he swam past them to the shady side and propped himself comfortably on a ledge. The brothers kept their steady gaze on the blonde as she did laps, their argument rising and falling in the gentle slap of the water.

Garth's wife called out, "It's 12 o'clock!" They arose in unison to pad back to their room and uncap their sanctioned beers. The water level in the pool seemed to lower appreciably. Cisco and Dion passed Garth and Rocky on the path, each giving the other the once over, each dismissing the other with unconscious snorts. "Ugly Americans," mouthed Dion to Cisco. "Java queers," Rocky said, rather too loudly to Garth.

In the pool Clive had already struck up a conversation with Raye, the blonde swimmer, who knew Cisco and Dion, waved and called hello. Raye, an American who'd lived at the villa for some months understood the peculiar rhythms of a small, isolated expatriate community that was neither rich nor tony, yet suffered the same ennui as the better resorts. She was a regular customer at Cisco and Dion's beauty shop in Lovina, as much for gossip as for scarlet toenails. When introduced to Clive as an artist, a painter, they said the usual things about wanting to see each other's work, but soon dropped networking talk in favor of the big question—what should Dion wear for his lip-sync debut at The Temple Saturday night? It was Friday, so they had the evening plus another whole day to ponder possibilities. They paddled around in the big blue pool, lazily enjoying the clear sunny day and cool water. Clive considered swimming-pool blue for the drapes in the Borges' living room. Rose-pink walls with the sparkle of a swimming-pool blue songket swag. Lovina was good for his muse.

"I can't decide between my gold shimmy-shimmy dress and the red one with spangles." Dion consulted with Raye, who appeared to be truly interested.

"Which wig?" she asked, apparently familiar with Dion's wardrobe. "The blonde Marilyn or shaggy Tina Turner?" Dion chewed his lip, pondering the question as though the correct answer would win him a refrigerator behind curtain number two. "I'm thinking—Tina?"

"Then do the shimmy-shimmy get-up with the Tina wig. Maybe throw on some sparkle dust," she suggested. "And red lips. Not maroon."

"Raye, that's brilliant! Yes, gold sparkle dust on the wig!" Dion's mood spiked appreciably, then downshifted. "Red lips, not maroon?" Still unsure.

Raye nodded encouragement, then turned to a new topic. "How's your little niece in Lombok? Still in school?" Dion forgot himself as he soared into his role as the dotting, rich uncle who sent money and sweets home to his family. He missed them, but they knew his career was important, and depended on the money he sent them.

Around 2 o'clock, Gede returned with three pots of purple orchids and a basket of mangosteen fruit. Everyone oohed over the orchids and gorged on the refreshing fruit, which had been cooled. "Look at this color," exclaimed Raye, breaking open the dusky purple shell of a mangosteen to reveal its fuchsia packaging. The pearly white fruit gleamed like teeth in the bright light. "Clive, you must find a way to use this color in something." She was right, it was a startling color, but one that demanded a certain restraint. Dion, who had no restraint, fashioned false lips out of the soft fuchsia stuff and blew smooches at Gede. "How about a kiss for the fuchsia?" he vamped. Clive grew annoyed, but everyone else laughed. He let it pass, then excused himself to shower and nap in the shade of his room.

Gede soon followed. Clive had the upstairs, Gede the daybed downstairs. Clive isolated himself in his curtained room, feeling vaguely unhappy. He fell into a shallow sleep and dreamed he was drowning. Gede held a fuchsia life preserver just out of his reach. He awoke to shouts in the courtyard.

"You dumb shit," growled a distinctly American voice. "This beer isn't even cold. You know what a cold beer is, don't you? It's a beer that is not un-cold." The sound of breaking glass followed; then a woman's loud sobs. Another American voice, slurred and mean, joined in. "Whadja expect, Garth? You got used goods, brother. Damaged merchandise."

"What the fuck do you know about being married, Rocky? Just what the fucking fuck do you know anyway?" Their voices drifted. The glass swept up, the wife's tears ignored. Clive could see Gede in the courtyard below keeping an eye on things. Clive glanced at his watch. Nearly 5 o'clock. Too early for dinner, but not too early for cocktails. He would rally the troops for an assault on the Sand Bar.

The rice farmers had chosen this morning to burn stubble left from harvested crops. The sky, gauzy with smoke, made Clive's hangover even more profound. Blue billows filled his already over-smoked lungs and made his eyes sting even before he opened them. Someone—that bloody South African—had talked him into drinking arak last night. Clive opened his eyes slowly, one at a time, but could not see. He tried to lie still and let his suffering bleed into his pillow. Even his pores ached.

Gede, Saint Gede, brought tepid tea, cool water, and four welcome tablets of Ibuprofen. When Clive awoke again it was early afternoon. He could hear a replay of yesterday's conversation in the pool with the troglodyte brothers. Perhaps there was something he could put in the pool, he thought weakly, or better, in their beer, something that would leave them incapable of speech. He dozed until sundown, awoke, and felt well enough to eat a little soup, then slept until after ten. He missed Dion's act at The Temple.

Clive asked Gede to take him back to Ubud. Gede moved about the room quietly, neatly packing Clive's clothes and arranging the potted orchids securely in the car. They drove home silently in the consoling dark. It was after midnight when they pulled into the driveway of Clive's bungalow. He suddenly felt lucid and sharply sober. "You drink arak, do you?" he asked Gede. "No, sir," replied Gede. "My cousin went blind from it." "Ah. Well then. No more of that."

His answering machine had two messages from Clarissa, one from an antique dealer, one from a potential client, a dentist from Darwin, the last one from Raye. She said it was urgent, to call right away. It was late. He hesitated, then punched in her number. It took awhile for her to be summoned from her room, to pick up the phone in the villa's office.

"Raye, you called?" He could hear a sharp intake of breath on the other end of the line. Raye spoke calmly at first. "Dion was murdered." A pause. "What? What did you say?" She continued, her voice gathering pressure, volume rising, words tumbling one upon the other. "Knifed with a *kreis*, two fingers cut off, seven stab wounds, in the back and heart. He went out for a smoke after his first set and didn't come back. Cisco found him in the alley. The police say they don't know who did it, of course. Maybe they will never know. It's not at the top of their investigation list. It's not that important, is it? Just one more gay boy. Dead. He must have known the games would end some day. Dion was just too good. When he put on his shimmy-shimmy dress and got all made up, he was the most beautiful girl in Bali."

"Oh God, Dion." She began to cry. "I'm so sorry, Clive. Dion was my friend. I know he was your friend, too. I'm so sorry. The doctor gave Cisco a sedative, he's sleeping now. I thought you should know." Clive clicked off the phone and held it in the palm of his hand as though he couldn't remember what it was for. He replaced it gently in the cradle. He turned to Gede.

Gede stood in the doorway between the hall and living room. In the transparent half light his silhouette etched a line of silver. He stood between the dark hall and the lighted room—a little more one way and his form would be whole.—less than a step back he would be swallowed by the dark. Invisible. The line into the darkness grew thin, barely a glimmer.

Oogah-Oogahs — Nyepi Puppets

Silence

The rainy season began, as everyone said it would, on November first, an even, drenching rain. Early on the downpours came twice or three times a week, then late in January, every day. Still, the heat did not abate. The newly planted rice fields simmered in steam. Sometimes in the afternoon a shimmering fog would hover over the fields like a sprinkle of glitter. Rain glossed and heightened the intensity of greens and blues in the banana trees and palms. Light pierced the clouds, running through sheets of green banana leaf with stripes of yellow and clear cerise that cast blue shadows that flowed like rivulets across the field.

After six months in Bali, Raye had finally learned how to live by herself. She had never before felt such freedom. She painted when she wanted, slept and ate when she felt tired or hungry. She had no other opinion to consider but her own. The numbness she felt after her lover wrote that he would not come to Bali gradually let go its grasp and at last she began to feel sensation return to her body. Raye told herself she didn't want a lover. Not that she didn't need one; she didn't want a lover.

Raye painted with fresh assurance, attempting unusual compositions. She had amassed a stack of paintings, but wanted a big body of work, more ideas to choose from before she sought out a gallery. She wasn't operating under her usual system of multi-layers of tasks and obligations. She wasn't marketing, writing grants, and teaching or giving slide shows, talking about theory and process. This newfound freedom allowed Raye a fresh approach to her art. She simply painted with one question in mind: Am I telling the truth? Truth didn't mean adhering to the dictates of the landscape, she could play with that as she wished, that was her right as an artist. Truth meant fidelity of feeling.

Raye felt a sudden need for change. She wanted to get agitated again, to move away from little routines she'd fixed on. If she had told herself the truth about the state of her desire as clearly as she told herself the truth about painting, she would have to admit she was lonesome. She consulted a map of Bali and planned a two-week sojourn to Candidasa for its charm as a ruined resort, and its accessibility to other destinations: Klungkung to the west, with 18th-century paintings of the Mahabharata at Kerta Gosa, the Hall of Justice, surrounded by a moat of pink water lilies; and Taman Ujung in the north, the Water Palace of the last regency's raja. Raye was also keen to visit Iseh, the mountain village where Walter Spies, a German artist, had built his country home in the 1930s with an uninterrupted view of Mt. Agung, Bali's highest volcano. Raye had seen Spies's work in Ubud at all the best museums. A European take on the Balinese paradise, of course, observed with particular awe and reverence for the exotic that outsiders have. Raye's paintings were nothing like Spies with his eerie, carefully composed views of Bali life, but she admired his sense of drama, his perspective.

At a secluded beach hotel, Raye unpacked her paints and set up temporary camp. The bungalows were built in the Balinese-style after rice huts and barns. Constructed from the wood of coconut and jackfruit trees, the bungalow walls were made from woven split bamboo, the furniture primitive carved teak. Her little beach bungalow was so airy it practically breathed. She could sit on her veranda and watch the sun dazzle the ocean. The violence of the sea invigorated her. To fill her gaze with the emerald-green Indian Ocean was enough.

It was also a pleasure to be in the company of other travelers: Hans, a Dutchman who lived alone at the largest, most remote bungalow in the compound for the past two months, fiercely defending his privacy. Taciturn and homely, with a large purple nose and small dark, darting eyes, he seemed proud of his ability to remain apart. Raye wondered why or how he could feel so pestered by the company of others. Still, he had been all over the island by himself and promised to give her suggestions for day trips. Half an hour of conversation was enough for him, she thought. He seemed completely exhausted by the effort, although he was friendly enough when they met again a few days later.

There were two outgoing couples from Germany as well, who stayed an extra week and invited her along for day excursions in their rented car. New people would come and go each day. It stimulated her to see changing faces, to have company for dinner. Then suddenly, the Hotel Kepala Kelapa was empty, or nearly so. A lone Swiss traveler, a honeymooning couple from the States who stayed inside their bungalow for two days, and Raye. Once again she breathed in her solitude and felt glad.

Raye found herself making quick sketches of the groundskeeper. At first she told herself her interest was aesthetic. She wanted to paint him. His teak-colored skin, his straight back, his black hair, and white teeth. He was from the Sudra caste, the lowest Hindu order, but he carried himself like a Brahmin. He was clever with wood and earth, building, fixing. Perhaps unworldly in Raye's Western experience, but in his world, in Bali, he knew how to read the landscape. He walked with a sharp curved *arit* tucked into the waist of his shorts. He worked instinctively, cutting, clearing, sweeping, stacking, climbing. His body moved with strength and confidence. His name was Kadek.

They talked. Raye questioned Kadek about his life, about Bali, the Hindu religion. He spoke English well, though not perfectly, not well enough to work in a big hotel. He helped her with Indonesian, happy to correct her pronunciation, to teach her. Raye felt she had made a friend. He told her how the land had been covered in coconut groves twenty years ago. His family lived right here, where the hotel stood now. His father had died in bungalow number four. His family wove mats out of grass. He had only three years of school. You mean three years of high school? asked Raye. No, three years of school. That's all.

When he laid his warm, brown hand firmly on the small of her back she instinctively leaned into it. Then she remembered that she was the American woman at the hotel and he was the groundskeeper. She told him to remove his hand. He did so without embarrassment. "Ma'af," he said, "Sorry," with what she interpreted as a slight bow, his eyes smiling. He was a few years younger than Raye; Kadek had already raised three kids. His wife had died two years ago. He seemed so old, yet young at the same time. He expounded upon his philosophies. He had ideas about strength, energy, karma. Raye listened and Kadek sat closer. Raye's two-week sojourn slipped into a month. She could not remember why she needed to go anywhere else.

Coconut harvesters came. The thud of dropping coconuts competed with crashing surf. They shimmied up a palm in seconds flat. Once in the fronds they lopped off the dead branches and young coconuts. Kadek supervised the process. The men gathered the coconuts and strung them together into bundles that were hoisted onto a bamboo pole that they balanced across their shoulders to take to the truck—the Balinese version of a strong man in a storybook circus. It rained, but they worked through it. Kadek came to Raye's bungalow, drenched, holding a gift. He took a coconut still encased in its golden husk, whacked a piece off the bottom with his arit so it would sit flat, made a hole in the top, put in a grass straw, and presented it to her. It was easy to be charmed.

The next day Raye came back to the bungalow in the late afternoon in the rain, this time she was the one drenched. Kadek said, "Let me bring you tea."

"Yes, " she agreed. "That would be lovely." She was taking a shower when he came back with the tea. She heard him approach and thought he'd leave it on the table on the veranda. He did. Then he walked into her room and slid open the bathroom door. She grabbed a towel, but he saw what he wanted. "Get out," she ordered. He backed out slowly. Yet Raye was moved by his intensity. She'd almost forgotten what lust felt like.

In the weeks before Nyepi, the Balinese New Year, *Oogah Oogah* suddenly appeared. Fashioned from split bamboo and paper, painted in vivid hues, great demon effigies began to sprout up in all the villages. The puppet-like statues were huge, some twelve-feet tall or more. Demon monkeys rode on papier-mâché motorcycles, and elephants carried leering henchmen. Other huge, hairy beasts wearing black-and-white checkered sarongs with clubs and kreis held high, their wicked expressions of delight lurked in alleyways or curtained workshops. In the nearby village of Sengkidu, the demon hag Rangda sported purple papaya-shaped breasts, and a malicious red grin as she waited for her turn at the crossroads. A wild party was about to happen.

At sunset a gamelan orchestra arrived at the temple gates of Sengkidu. After a short session of prayers and offerings, a pack of young men hoisted the effigy of Rangda with her wild black hair, tusks, and lolling tongue, onto a palanquin, and marched off down the dark street, making a racket with drums and cymbals and shouts. They tossed the creature about and spun around at every corner. The street flickered into view in little glimpses illuminated by torches held aloft by men and boys. No visible moon, only stars lit the night sky.

The women, dressed in lacey blouses and colorful sarongs, balanced offerings of fruit and flowers on their heads. They were absorbed into the throng. Raye marched along with the crowd, up one side of the road, and down the other, circling back to the temple. Boys beat bamboo sticks together ferociously to raise the din. Men with brass cymbals crashed their instruments together with ruthless energy. Some knelt, as though in prayer close to the ground, others reached high above their heads exalting their instruments in a deafening crescendo.

Everyone gathered around the Oogah Oogah in the temple courtyard. A boy stuck a torch into the mouth of the monster. Rangda's paper head went up in a magnificent plume of sparks. As the smoke blew toward the ocean, Raye could see Kadek's face lit by flame through the disintegrating skeleton. He saw her, too, and moved through the crowd to her. She did not turn away. They walked in silence through the dark back to the hotel. Raye opened the door to her bungalow. She knew if she let Kedek cross the threshold she would not be able to turn back.

As soon as they were in the room, Kadek bolted the door, closed the shutters, and pulled her to him, his hands everywhere, grasping, tearing at her. She faltered, pushed him away, but her body said yes, and he knew it. She could feel him hard under his sarong, everything about him wound tight. He was all fever and want. His kisses were indistinct, his hands too, not really feeling but clutching her. He was aggressive, almost violent. They did not say a word to each other as they tussled. Finally, she insisted he must go. He reluctantly released her and allowed himself to be pushed out the back door. Raye rested her cheek against the cool bamboo and smiled. There were a thousand reasons why he should not be her lover—only one why he should.

The next day was Nyepi, the Day of Silence. No cars or motorbikes allowed on the road, no airplanes in the sky across the island. No electricity permitted, no fires lit. It was forbidden to leave the hotel compound. If you did, you were in danger of being stoned by local Security. A blissfully quiet day, cloudy and rainy most of the time. People spoke to each other in whispers. Even the roosters crowed softly. Everyone said it was lucky that it had rained—a good omen, a cleansing spirit.

Kadek came to Raye's bungalow and stood in the doorway, open-faced, sincere. "Ma'af," he said, "I am sorry about last night. You make me crazy. I am in love with you, Raye. I think you want me, too." He said this simply as though it were all up to her to decide their fate. A surge of hope ran alongside Raye's newfound feelings of desire. Hope that canceled out all reason and doubt. That they could not really understand each other's language, or culture, or ideas about religion was, in this misty light, no barrier. That she had nearly fifteen more years of schooling than he, did not seem a problem. That he had grown children, that he made less than $500 a year, was no problem, tidak apa apa. Only this moment mattered. Everything else seemed to be simply the stuff and noise of life, not the energy of life, which was this one thing only—to love and be loved.

In this rationalization of her irrational self there loomed other, bigger doubts that as soon they appeared, simply floated away like balloons at a parade. His love-making, his fury would not satisfy her. She knew this from his first kiss. His smell was deep, feral, intense. He sought to take from her, to wound her with his sex, when what she desired, what she craved, was a lover who could match her kisses, to reply in kind. Raye studied Kadek's face and could find no doubt in him. His desire was direct. All these thoughts came crashing through the door of Raye's solitude. Her carefully constructed sense of permanent aloneness dissolved in the heat of his need and her loneliness. That it would turn out badly, that they would wound each other in such imaginatively cruel ways was unimportant now. It was Nyepi, the Day of Silence. They had no need for words.

Badung Berlayar — Badung Strait

The Last Tourist in Bali

Adam Mark stopped to look at the sea. He watched himself look as if viewing a film with a voice over. "Okay," he said, taking inventory: "Cerulean with ultramarine thinned to cobalt green. No cobalt blue in the picture at all." The water broke endlessly into discrete fragments of color, then continuously mixed itself into a new shade. He used to know how to see. It was easy—he'd simply let his vision go out of focus, just a tiny bit, so he could see what the thing was made of. Then he could put it all back together again on the canvas. Not the thing itself—not as an ocean or an apple or a kite, but abstracted, larger and more poetic than the real thing. The "more poetic than the real thing" was a remembered quote from an old review. Adam shook his head as he tapped out a cigarette, sat on the stone wall overlooking the beach and tried again to see. *See the sea,* a little sing-song voice prattled in his head. *See the sea.* The problem was in the seeing. He could take it apart, analyze the pieces, but could not put it back together. He could not see it anymore.

He lit a cigarette with a match, contemplating the chromatic range caught in the flame as he gently inhaled. He let the smoke drift from his mouth, drew it back in through his nose, slowly sending twin wisps of blue into the pale sky. Clove-scented tobacco numbed his mouth, made him feel calmer.

No big deal, he reasoned. Just because it used to be easy, doesn't mean a thing now. As a painter he belonged to a quaint profession, practically archaic. Modern artists worked with concepts, and other people's money, his wife had told him. When he had a wife. He should be designing airports, working with lasers and computers, and the latest technology, she said. Except that he didn't care about any of that. What did he care about? Hard to recall. He changed. Something got lost on the way to the bank. Now he is in Bali, about as far away from L.A. as he could imagine. "Remote," a word his wife once used to describe him. She also said he was like an island, but she never accused him of being a tropical island. Adam squinted at the sea, flattening the mass into a stripe more green than blue. Nothing to do but see the sea. He smoked and looked out at the horizon. Exotic Bali. Not so remarkable anymore. Not so exotic after two months. Just an island surrounded by water that sometimes looked blue, sometimes green. On the best days, gray, silver-gray. His favorite color now.

A local kid pulled up on a motorbike, a vinyl case bungied behind him. The kid pushed his mirrored, wraparound sunglasses up so they held back his long black hair like a headband. Smiling, he approached Adam as though they were old friends.

"Watches?" the kid said hopefully. "Watches, watches?" opening the case that displayed neat rows of plastic wrapped watches. "Rrrolex?" he said giving the "r" a soft Indonesian purr. "Gucci? Calvin Clean? Cheap, cheap?" The eternal question. "Nah," growled Adam, not even looking at the proffered goods. He stubbed out his cigarette on the wall. "I don't have time for fucking watches."

The kid didn't register the joke, if it was a joke. Adam himself did not know. He had one mood now: silver-gray. He wasn't sure if this bothered him or not. He turned to go. The kid, undeterred by his surly customer, tried a new approach. He flipped the case around and opened the other side. "Sunglasses?" he asked hopefully. "Ray Bon?" he pleaded. Adam did not reply. He turned his back to the kid and walked away.

It must be late afternoon by the length of the palm tree shadows, he guessed. Funny how many locals were selling watches when free time was in such abundance. No one here really knew what time it was anyway. You could ask half a dozen people in the village and get six different answers. Locals, expats, tourists all entered this demilitarized timezone. Day or night, that was all that mattered. Day meant light and the plague of seeing. Day was more complicated than night—there was the long morning to contend with, then the afternoon. The early afternoon heat could be obliterated with a short nap, but then the awful shimmering colors of late afternoon light would taunt him. The light was so exquisite it was painful. Night meant dark and the relief of forgetting. Adam walked back to his bungalow looking at the ground, measuring his steps, marking time until night would arrive.

Dewa shifted a small canvas on the floor to catch the remaining light. He painted stylized tufts of pale-pink clouds on a solid blue sky. In his family, he was the cloud-man. His older brother, Wayan, blocked in masses of flat color that would become jungle, priests, monkeys, or kids flying kites. Wayan was the color-man. His younger brother, Nadi, finished the painting by outlining the figures with a thin edge of black and highlighting foliage with flicks of bright green or yellow. He was the line-man. Dewa did the clouds, foliage, and flowers. The middle-man, the detailer, as he was in the family. They produced paintings in the Young Artists Style, which developed in the early '60s under the guidance of Arie Smit, a Dutchman who became a naturalized Indonesian and started his own school near the art center of Ubud. Now the Young Artists Style was recognized as a Balinese art, practiced by schools and family ateliers for the tourist trade. Dewa called himself a painter, not an artist. Painting was easy. Selling the paintings used to be easy, too, but now there weren't so many tourists. Dewa believes they will come back. He prays and makes offerings to the temple. He gives flowers to the gods and rice to the demons. Everyone must have their fair share. His family still owns rice fields and coconut groves. They will eat; they have enough.

Dewa chased the light until it slid out the door. He cleaned his brush on an old T-shirt and leaned the painting against the wall to dry. He looked out over the rice fields at the fading sky, recognizing his pale-pink clouds in the distance.

Adam sat on his veranda as the dark settled in. The mosquitoes didn't bother him so much anymore. As color drained from the sky, Adam smoked and waited. He wondered if this was happiness—to be alone, to do nothing, to be nobody. He could not be sure; he needed confirmation. When the first star showed, Adam would head for the Gecko, a thatched-roof bar down on the beach. The band had just finished the opening set. Adam nodded to Dewa, who joined him at the bar. "Wayan is wailing tonight!" Dewa exclaimed.

Adam smiled for the first time that day. Wailing Wayan sang like an angel. He was shorter than his younger brother Dewa, and his black hair was longer. He had a silky voice made for the blues with an indefinite sexuality that appealed to both men and women. Dewa and his brothers played the Gecko three nights a week. They did not invent, played nothing original, covered old rock 'n' roll and blues, some new Indonesian pop tunes, but they all had pretty voices, and they loved playing.

Adam offered Dewa a cigarette.

"Man, you are one ambitious Indonesian." Adam said this as a compliment.

Dewa corrected him, "I am Balinese, man, Balinese first, then Indonesian. And what do you mean 'ambitious'?"

Adam did not intend to offend his friend. "I just meant you have two gigs—painter by day, musician by night. Plus farmer, father, member of the council. You got a lot going on. Not like those watch sellers who hang out all day, waiting for the lone, unsuspecting tourist. You get out there. You don't stand in one place. It's good. You got American instincts. Ambitious."

Dewa knew Adam was praising him, but did not care for the compliment. Ambitious meant you wanted too much. Ambitious meant greedy. It was an affront to the gods to be ambitious. He didn't want anything. "I paint because that is what we do in my family. I play music because it is fun." Dewa's English was excellent, but he didn't understand what Adam was getting at.

"Yeah," said Adam, "but I've got to ask you about those paintings. I mean how do you do it . . . keep it going? Doesn't that inky-dinky stuff get to you after awhile? Aren't you bored with doing the same shit over and over again? What would you paint if it was just you and the canvas?"

Dewa wondered if Adam was already

drunk. He wasn't usually this talkative. "I paint the way we have always painted. It's good if it sells. It sells because it fits the style. We all know this. If it was just me and the canvas, I don't know. I probably wouldn't paint at all."

Like me, thought Adam. He tried to smile. He ordered another round of Bintangs for them both. "It's just strange to me. I would never share a canvas with someone, even my brother. Especially my brother." Adam faced Dewa, serious. "I don't know. It's got to be my own, belong to me. Just me."

Dewa took a long look at his friend. "Are we talking about Beauty again?" he began, but Adam waved him off, not in the mood for another discussion about the cultural differences between West and East. What did it matter? Play on! Have another beer.

Adam shrugged and turned his back to the bar, leaned against the ledge and looked out at the crowd. Not really enough to call them a crowd: a knot of over-baked middle-aged tourist women—a big redhead caught his eye and winked. Two Aussie expats, without their wives, getting shit-faced. That American woman who's been here a long time with a new guy. Someone said she was an artist. Probably a watercolorist. He didn't want to know. And Ketut's girlfriend with another smiling Balinese girl. More locals would probably show up after nine. At least they weren't all Germans or Dutch tonight he thought gratefully, remembering the All Requests Night when the Schmidt family reunion wanted nothing but Iron Butterfly.

Adam felt good now. The beer buzz loosened tightness in his shoulders and he stopped thinking about painting. He waved to Ketut's girlfriend, what was her name? And that other girl he hadn't noticed before. Her cousin, Dewa said. He asked Dewa to introduce him. The girls, silly and shy, twittered behind their hands held up like fans, with Cokes on the table meant to last all evening. Introductions made, ("Of course, I remember, Lila, right? And Tini? I'm Adam. Cigarette?") Adam made a goofy attempt at a joke about Tini's name being as diminutive as she was. The joke did not translate. The girls laughed anyway. Dewa left to join the band tuning up for their next set.

Tini did not smoke. Or drink. Nice Balinese girls didn't. At least not in public. Charming, thought Adam. American girls wouldn't make that effort. Wouldn't let you call them girls either. Tini seemed to be warming to him. He bought them ice cream, a huge plate of pink and yellow and brown globs to share. The girls giggled and nibbled and let the whole mess melt into a great multi-colored puddle. Adam chased the drips with a tine of his fork, spiraling it into whorls on the smooth plank table. For a few minutes he forgot about the girls, and the music, and why he wasn't painting, lost in the process of turning viscous matter into form. Lila and Tini silently watched him as they would a strange bug. Adam snapped out of his reverie and blotted his creation with a paper napkin. He pulled his chair back so he could observe Tini while pretending to listen to the band.

She was young, maybe too young. but affected MTV independence with tight jeans and a midriff-skimming top. She kept her hair long, fiddling with it, tying it into a knot and jamming a great toothy clip into the center to hold it back, then shaking it free again. Her hair, so shiny, like water. Adam wanted to touch it. *Not yet.* He bobbed his chin to the music just as she turned for a glimpse at him. He feigned indifference, but noticed how dark her eyes were. Was she wearing make-up? He couldn't tell. Her lips were so rosy and moist. He wanted to taste them. *Not yet.* He lit another cigarette, reached across the table for the ashtray as his fingers brushed against her arm, the color of caramel, smooth and hairless, no rings or bracelets. Naked. He wanted to put his mouth on her wrist, to feel the throb of her pulse. *Not yet.* She did not move away from his touch. He had no idea what song the band was playing, but he wanted to dance with her. *Not yet, not yet.*

Adam could see himself sliding into this—what would you call it?—relationship? No, that was too complicated. He wanted to touch her, to make love to her, that was all. He'd been on the island for two months locked into his old miseries and regrets, bored with himself. He came here for Beauty, and now this vision appeared before him at the Gecko. He wanted to sleep with her. Not yet. Not tonight. But soon. Tini smiled at Adam, showed her straight white teeth and dark sympathetic eyes.

❦

In and out of bed, Tini didn't talk much. She surrendered to his touch, so cool and smooth, docile, and sweet, that was enough. He wasn't really curious about her. Adam's problems with painting began to fade. He didn't even try. He slept more during the day, drank more at night, and now had Tini to occupy his other senses. He relaxed into the rhythm of the tropics. A simple life. One day she asked for a small favor. Her sister needed a little money for school books. It wasn't much. Adam gave it to her freely. Then, her uncle needed to see a doctor, her cousin needed a school uniform, her mother needed offerings for the ancestors. Adam didn't complain. He had enough money. More than enough. She never asked for anything for herself. She was so easy to please.

Adam wanted to surprise her, give her a treat. He suggested Tini come with him on a shopping trip to Denpasar. They could go to Matahari, the big department store, and she could buy new clothes or something else for herself. Whatever she wanted. Adam liked the idea of taking her out, showing her off, spoiling her a little. Tini would be so grateful—with that cool, innocent look she wore so well. Tini, quietly nodded yes, she would like to go on the shopping trip, but asked if her cousin could come with them. Sure. Better, in fact. Shopping with a woman could test even the strongest man's stamina. Cousin. He thought he heard the singular, but four girls waited on the corner to pile into the boxy Toyota he hired for the day. Okay, no problem. Let there be a party.

The girls jabbered nonstop all the way to the city. They spoke in Balinese, of which Adam knew not one word. Still, they were all so pretty and chirpy, they fussed and flirted with him. He carried them in the air-conditioned car right up to the doorstep of their dreams. Once inside they moved as a gang, pawing through racks of synthetic clothes, T-shirts in lurid colors with rhinestones and misspelled television celebrity names, impossibly tight, airbrushed jeans, and vinyl, opened-toed sandals with cork heels. The sales clerks bagged the merchandise and handed Adam the receipt. "Not yet," smiled Tini. "Pay later," as she steered her entourage up the escalator into home goods. They systematically razed the shelves of plasticware, tumblers with unlicensed cartoon characters, plates and bowls in florescent green and pink with snap-on lids, something that resembled a large, curved fork and an electric rice cooker with a Pennsylvania Dutch tulip motif. It was all so cheap, how could he say no? Tini spied a plastic gold-framed mirror, enraptured with its faux-baroque elegance. Why not? More things: baby shoes that lit up and squeaked, a big jar of Mentos, a Hello Kitty pencil case, gigantic sparkly hair clips. Everything appealed to Tini and her mob of cousins. Finally, they were exhausted. Downstairs all of the parcels miraculously awaited his MasterCard signature. The bill came to two million three hundred thousand rupiah, $267. Adam had expected more; still he felt queasy.

Tini and her cousins cradled their plastic bags of stuff like precious babies. They were talked-out on the way home. Adam dropped Tini and her cousins at the family compound, told her he'd see her later, and slunk home, stunned. It wasn't the cost of the things; he'd spent as much buying CDs in a weekend in L.A., once upon a time. It wasn't even the volume they amassed that bothered him. It was the junk itself—cheap and ugly, synthetic and neon-colored. They were living on an island known for its beauty—magnificent ancient temples with exquisitely carved wooden gates and stone statuary, traditional batik and songket weavings, finely wrought silverwork. Even the daily ephemeral offerings at every home and temple—the tiny green baskets made from palm or banana leaf decorated with artful arrangements of flowers and fruit, had lulled Adam into believing that all Balinese were born with an innate sense of Beauty. Suddenly he realized his girlfriend was the leader of a gang whose credo was to accumulate a mass of hideous stuff. He had to think this over. This beautiful girl, this perfect caramel sweet, his girlfriend, had absolutely appalling taste. This was news to him. He'd known her for a month and had never noticed.

Adam opened a fresh Bingtang and sat on his veranda overlooking the sea. It was changing color. Not quite green or blue, more turquoise, but not so deep as that. Translucent as glass. Sea glass. Why was he here? Because L.A. sucked. Because his wife left him. Because his last show was panned. Not real reasons. Excuses, maybe. He came to Bali to reclaim his art. To renew his senses. To rediscover

Beauty. Yet, he could not paint. He did not want to say this aloud. Until this moment, he thought he'd found Beauty with his Tini—so smooth, unspoiled, innocent. He had almost felt inspired by her, almost wanted to paint her. Now all that passed like a sigh from the center of his desire. None of it true. He had no idea about Beauty now. He had no idea who this girl was that he'd been making love to. He looked into the future and it looked crowded with cheap, ugly stuff. The sea itself a crude cliché—a postcard parody of paradise. He had to get away.

Dewa tried to paint with his baby girl on his lap. She cooed and gurgled, pulled his hair, climbed up to his shoulder as he bent to fill in the last of the banana trees in the picture. She dug her scratchy little toes into his ribs, which made him jump and left a blob of green where there should have been blue. Still unperturbed, he shifted her to his other hip while he found a rag to correct the mistake.

His brother Nadi hummed to himself as he sat crossed-legged in a square of sunshine at the other end of the room, hunched over a canvas with a tiny brush outlining foliage from the last series. His older brother had already left for the day.

Adam's shadow appeared in the doorway. Dewa greeted him pleasantly, happy to take a break. He handed the squirming child to Adam while he fixed the painting. Adam, not used to children, especially babies, held her uneasily. The baby tried her best to charm him, opening her round eyes wide with curiosity and sucking on her tiny brown fist, making little bird sounds. Adam observed her, un-charmed, relieved when Dewa took her back. They went outside to smoke under the Banyan tree.

"Remember that little island you told me about? The one off Nusa Penida? I want to go there," said Adam. He smoked impatiently. "Can you take me?"

"But no one is there this time of year," countered Dewa. "The rainy season is coming. It's very isolated. I don't know, my friend."

"That's what I need, man. It's getting too crowded here, too many distractions. I've got to get away, get some perspective."

Dewa smoked without comment, the baby dozed in his arms. Finally, he spoke, giving Adam the facts: the most direct route would be to take a ferry to Pandang Bai to the main port and hire a local boat to the smaller island. Adam adamantly opposed this suggestion. He wanted Dewa to find a boatman to take them. He needed Dewa as his guide, his translator. Dewa finally nodded his agreement, but cautioned Adam it could take awhile to arrange everything. He would let him know when the time was right. Not tomorrow. It might be a week or so. Adam went back to the beach confident he had a plan at last. He bought a case of Bingtang beer and waited in his bungalow.

By the time Dewa had found a boat to take them to the island almost two weeks had passed and the rainy season had begun in earnest. They delayed the voyage another day because of the weather, then a sudden bright morning graciously granted easy passage. From Pandang Bai the ferry would take less than two hours to get to the main port. In the little fishing boat Dewa hired it would probably be twice that, plus a little more to get to the village. Dewa agreed to accompany Adam and introduce him to his friend who would rent him a hut on the south side, and would come back with the boatman the next day. Dewa felt glad for the trip and extra money, the "trekkers fee" Adam insisted upon. His family could get along without him for a day. Anyway, not much point in painting pictures that no one would even look at, let alone buy this time of year. The Gecko wanted the band only one night a week now, and they played for theoretical tips. No tourists. The village wasn't asleep, it was in a coma.

They sat in a line on planks in the narrow pink boat, with Adam's seven bags of books and paints and canvas weighing down the stern. The boatman, a cousin of Dewa's, revved up the tiny gas engine and nosed it south of Nusa Penida, which glowed faintly blue on the horizon. Dewa watched Adam's intent expression that never relaxed as the boat picked up speed. Okay, my friend, he thought with a smile, you want a place with no distractions, I will show it to you. Past the swells, the boatman put up the sail, shut off the motor, and let the wind push them out to sea. The breeze was steady, no clouds in sight. Just the rhythmic slap and lift of the boat moving with the waves. Dewa brought out rice wrapped in banana leaf his wife had prepared for the trip. They ate in silence, then offered the wrappings to the Baruna, god of the sea. A school of silver, pencil-sized fish surrounded the boat in a churning mass, then abruptly departed. The sail flapped in sync with the waves.

They'd rounded the first headland when the wind abruptly shifted. Dewa scrambled to collapse the sail, but the boat went into a spin, dipping and bucking in the sudden waves. Thick clouds thundered in, light left the sky. It happened so quickly, the boat filled with water so fast it just seemed to melt into the sea. The boatsman could not swim at all, and Dewa could barely keep his head above the water. No one wore life vests. The two Balinese clung to the sinking boat for as long as they could. Sharp rain sliced the water. The mast snapped free and ducked out of sight with the next swell. The boatsman let go of the hull first, with a startled half-wave slipped from view. Adam called out to Dewa to hold on, but it was impossible to see anything in the crashing black water. When he looked again Dewa had vanished. He called to Dewa over and over, although he could not hear his own voice. Crosscurrents pulled him one way, then another. Adam instinctively tucked in his head and swam toward the shore.

The water was not cold, but thick, heavy.

Adam attempted to part it again and again, pulling the shore closer to him with each stroke. He swam without seeing, without thought or feeling until at last sand under his feet brought him upright onto the beach. As soon as his feet touched the shifting ground he became aware of the sound of the storm. Thunder, rolling thunder as monotonous as the pounding waves. Relentless wind a shrill counterpart to the deep drone of rain. The black sky continued its assault. Adam found partial shelter under a banana tree, the water a translucent wall on three sides. He scanned the horizon. No sign of Dewa or the boatsman. No sign of the boat.

The rain let up at sunset when the sky split open, transformed into hot gold, lava-red and molten. Adam could see the parts, the construction, but now he knew how to put it back together. He understood the vividness of the sky could be rendered so only by contrast of a becalmed black sea. The dark offset the brilliance of light. Without that dark stripe on the horizon, the red-orange had no meaning. Adam could finally see it, he understood. Beauty was so simple. He watched the sky fade and merge with the black sea. Bright stars pricked though the canopy one by one until the sky spun with multi-colored whirls of light. The flat sea mirrored the night sky, twin disks of dazzling light. Adam felt the light penetrate his vision, soak into his bones. At last, he pulled a banana leaf around him like a shawl, pillowed his head in the palm of his hand, and slept a deep and dreamless sleep.

Acknowledgements

Grateful thanks to my Balinese friends who shared their customs and culture with me: Ketut, Wayan, Gede, and Nadi.

Many thanks to my first editor, Tim Lange, who made me feel like I had something to say. Humble thanks to my editor and publisher at Baksun Books, Jennifer Heath, for her smarts. And to my first readers, S.D. Hall and Niko Murry.

Eternal thanks to to my mentor Lucia Berlin. And to my Naropa teachers: Jack Collom, Bobbie Louise Hawkins, and Anne Waldman. Reverential thanks to Saraswati, Hindu Goddess of Books and Creativity.

Special thanks to my expatriate friends in Chiang Mai, Carl and Keiko Samuels, and Yamini Mishiri, for places to write. And to Cynthia Thacker, back in the States, for solitude at the Avila beachhouse to do re-writes.

Loving thanks to my Boulder tribe: Cha Cha, Madhavii Shirman, and Sherry Hart for support and encouragement through the years. To my son Damian Sky Lauria, for accompanying me on the first part of the journey to Bali. And to Ken Bernstein, for his loving heart.

About the Author

photo by Cha Cha

TREE BERNSTEIN recently spent two years as a Peace Corps Volunteer, teaching English and art in Cambodia (2015-17). Previously, she taught writing and literature at the Brooks Photography Institute for over a decade.

Bernstein's work has been anthologized in *Thus Spake the Corpse—An Esquiste Corpse Reader; Low Down & Coming On! Poems About Pigs; If Bees Are Few—a Hive of Bee Poems; Askew Poetry Journal*; and other journals and magazines. Her first book of short stories, *On the Way Here*, was published by Baksun Books in 1997.

Before serving in the Peace Corps, Bernstein was Ventura Area Coordinator for California Poets in the Schools and poetry coach for Poetry Out Loud. She holds a MFA in Writing & Poetics from Naropa University and lives in Colorado.

Baksun Books

BAKSUN BOOKS was founded by Jennifer Heath in 1992, as a small press dedicated to de-commodifying the word, and, in 1994 began creating educational and topical art exhibitions.

Baksun Books is dedicated to bringing people together to find strategies for confronting today's issues, illustrating and contextualizing them to highlight the beauty of our natural and cultural gifts and resources, and to heal. The arts not only "speak truth to power," but uphold that truth and carry it forward. The mission of Baksun Books & Arts (fiscally sponsored by the Boulder County Arts Alliance) is to produce imaginative projects, publish books of poetry and prose, and curate art exhibitions—frequently on behalf of social and environmental justice—accompanied by comprehensive exhibition catalogs.

Baksun attempts to examine issues from as many creative and interactive angles as possible in the firm conviction that the arts can influence change.

Selected Baksun Titles

Exhibition Catalogs

Curated by Jennifer Heath

Celebration! A History of the Visual Arts in Boulder
Imaginary Maps: Expeditions to Uncover Apocryphal, Unsubstantiated & Forbidden Places
Uncontained: Writers & Photographers in the Garden & the Margins
The Veil: Visible & Invisible Spaces
Water, Water Everywhere: Paean to a Vanishing Resource

Prose, Poetry & Miscellany

La Niña, Urban Fairytales, Book One: Paperdoll, Sarah Bell
On The Way Here: Stories, Tree Bernstein
Addled Smoke Material: Collaborative Poems 1972 2017, Reed Bye & Jack Collom
Oleku Laku Biar: Mistranslations From the Basque, Jack Collom
The Task, Jack Collom
On Laughter: A Melodrama, Lyn Hejinian & Jack Collom
Wild West Wind: Remembering Allen Ginsberg, Susan Edwards
A Life In Pencil: Poems, Ghada Kanafani
How I Learned To Cook: An Artist's Life, Barbara Shark
Lump Gulch Tales, Jane Wodening
The Inside Story, Jane Wodening
Where Hunger is a Place: Poems, Laura Wright

Made in the USA
Monee, IL
12 February 2020

21555981R00098